SPARROW

APRIL SUNSHINE

Copyright © 2025 by Chicken House Press and April Sunshine

This book is a work of fiction. Unless otherwise indicated, all the names, characters, places, events and incidents in this book are either the product of the author's imagination or used in a fictitious manner. Any resemblance to actual persons, living or dead, or actual events is purely coincidental.

All rights reserved. This book or any portion thereof may not be reproduced or used in any manner whatsoever without the express written permission of the publisher except for the use of brief quotations in a book review or scholarly journal.

First Printing: 2025
CHICKEN HOUSE PRESS

Library and Archives Canada Cataloguing in Publication
CIP data on file with the National Library and Archives

ISBN trade paperback edition: 978-1-990336-85-0

Chicken House Press
282906 Normanby/Bentinck Townline
Durham, Ontario, Canada, N0G 1R0
www.chickenhousepress.ca

To anyone who picked up this book and gave it a chance… thank you! For that and for not skipping the dedication page!

SPARROW

APRIL SUNSHINE

When twilight gleams come what may
To wash away another day
Yet in the dark the shadows play
Tossing secrets of truth and lie
Twisting, dancing, refusing to fly
Away with the sun to the land of dreams
Lying in wait for the first ray to gleam
While at rest and peace outshines a light
Be content in yourself tonight
For tomorrow is another day
Believe in yourself
And the truth may decide to stay…

CHAPTER ONE

The darkness threatened to swallow her. It surrounded her, flooding every sense. Tight forces held her suspended in the air as she fought against invisible binds. Urgently grasping for something to hold onto—a ledge to bring her to safety. Fear travelled up her spine and she dreaded what would come next. Choking on desperation, her breathing increased as the haunting screams began. Pressure shoved her blood upwards, pounding at her skull as she cried for the echoing yells to stop. The high pitched cries grew sharper and louder. The pit in her gut affirming it was hopeless, there was no way out, no end to the black hole she was locked in. Feeling her heart leap to her throat as her stomach dropped, she fell into the darkness, into the never-ending pain, into…

Ro's eyes shot open and she exhaled with a jagged hiss. It was that stupid nightmare again. Heavy covers tangled around her as the cool floor braced her sweaty back. The bed was only a few feet above, pillows and sheets strewn about from her obvious distress as she fought to escape the dream she had been stuck in. Drenched in sweat and in urgent need of water, she forced herself to stand on shaky legs, pushing back her bushy red hair from her eyes. A chill raced down her spine and she spun around to look at the window across the room. Wispy smoke danced in the wind as candle wax pooled around the edge of a crystalline glass. Still unsteady, Ro walked over and closed the window with a slam, bringing down the curtain with a shiver. It could be the nightmare talking, but she felt like eyes had been peering at her from the darkened yard, although one quick look reassured her no one was there. Wrapping an arm around her stomach, she yanked her phone from the charger, and headed downstairs to the kitchen.

Seven sharp chimes of an old grandfather clock mixed with the sun rising brightly through her living room windows. At this hour, the house would normally dance as some cheesy mellow playlist accosted her ears. This morning, it was oddly quiet—no music or sizzling food. Now that she thought of it, not even the normal twittering of birds out by the water. It seemed eerily silent, but she quickly shook off that thought as she filled a glass with water. It was, after all, the first morning Althea was not home, the first morning since the accident Ro had truly been left alone.

Eight months ago, everything had gone as black as her dreams. She couldn't remember any of it. They told her the day had begun as a normal Sunday, but had turned into something much different, an atrocious event that had been ripped from her memory. Two days were missing; not one foggy recollection to rely on. Remembering was like trying to pull a tightened cord out of water, with something on the other end tugging against her, refusing to surface. She could still feel the pain from the blinding hospital lights as her eyes met Althea's focused gaze when she first woke up.

Her gut had screamed that something was wrong. Ro felt empty, numb, and locked in a haze. She soon realized everything was gone — her family, her friends — her life was forever changed. Against the sound of a beeping monitor, she had tried to pull one single moment from the previous two days to mind. All that came were mundane reminders she had given herself to switch the laundry and plans for a movie night with Adyra, a get-together she was told never happened. Throughout the doctor's questions, MRIs, and blood work she fought to hide her erupting panic, but no matter how hard she strained, no memories surfaced from the time lost.

"Lacunar amnesia," a stiff doctor had grunted to her and the tall detective who had been asking all the questions. A gap in her memory, they said, usually related to a specific event or period. "The trauma's the main factor in her amnesia." He had shrugged. "It's often temporary though."

That's when Althea calmly explained there had been some sort of accident leading to the bandage wrapped around Ro's head. From the neighbour's accounts, a deafening boom had shaken the ground and cut the electricity. Shortly after, authorities slid into the driveway, spraying gravel all over the shattered wood that had once stood as a home. Alone, Ro had laid in the rubble. No one else was found.

"As the closest thing you have to kin, you'll go home with Mrs. Althea upon discharge. If you remember anything, anything at all, you are to tell her immediately and she will contact me."

"And my parents?" Ro had shakily asked.

"Leave that investigation up to us; when we find them, Althea will let you know."

Ro had refused to let him leave until he twice repeated the reassuring promise that he would reach out soon.

Yet, time went on, as it often does, and spring turned into summer, followed by a cold winter that revealed no answers to any of the burning questions, and no hint of the memories she had lost. Eight long months of living with Althea on the isolated Claudaith Island. Ro pushed all the confusion and pain into a dark, locked box in her brain.

She tried to ignore it, but every now and then that box would threaten to burst open, especially when she would catch Althea staring at her with a look—not of pity, but a fearful curiosity. This look was striking and unfamiliar, especially for the small, older woman who had taken her in.

Her godmother was quiet and sweet, never pushing Ro too hard when it came to remembering that dreadful day, and always around to calm her terror. She was the perfect example of a generous person, caring with a motherly instinct. Althea had never had any children before the divorce from Ro's godfather, Peri, but Ro knew Althea would have been the best mother. She was someone who Ro knew she could always rely on; but today, Althea was gone.

She hadn't wanted to leave, but a potential business meeting required her absence. With Ro's promise to text her throughout the day and call if there was an emergency, Althea had departed down the overgrown trail that would lead her to the ferry on the east side of the island. Even though Ro wanted to sink into the disappointment that Althea leaving would mean she was alone for her 19th birthday, she held onto the gratitude of being able to have a small celebration with Althea the morning of her departure. As much as she wanted to throw a pity party, Ro knew that something was better than nothing.

As she walked to the couch, water splashed onto her hand from the glass she'd overfilled, jolting her out of her thoughts. Wiping the moisture on her faded jeans, she pulled her phone out of her back pocket, ready to settle into a comfy position and use the mind-numbing escape of technology to ignore her fears. The dream had scared her; it always did. Leftover remnants of icy dread lingered in her veins. Ro pushed the thoughts down to the part of her brain where she could pretend they didn't exist.

It was way too early to be awake. Her eyes begged

for more sleep as she swallowed a lump of anxiety and swiped at the screen to check her messages. Claudaith didn't provide much signal and the Wi-Fi was just shy of crappy, but she made do with that she had.

The screen contrasted with the unlit room and burned her eyes for a moment until her pupils adjusted to the dawn leaking through the windows. Clearing useless notifications and scrolling through poorly loading social media, one new message brought a smile to her face.

The screen flashed neon. "Happy Birthday girl!"

Adyra had always made it a point to wish her a happy birthday no matter where they were, yet Ro was surprised to see a message at all this time. After the first three months of unanswered texts and calls, Ro had all but given up on hearing from her best friends. Adyra's non-responsiveness in a time where Ro's whole world was falling apart was an uncharted landscape. She guessed her loud-spoken friend might not have found the words to say in such a trying time. It was Adyra's parents who had called the police that day; maybe she just needed some more time.

Ace, Ro's other lifelong friend, had stiffly responded to her messages only once. "Stop texting me." It was enough to get his harsh point across.

Ro typed out a quick thank you to Adyra's unexpected message and moved on to let Althea know her plans for the day. To prevent the sadness creeping behind her eyes from overwhelming her, she fought to focus on the everyday normalcies of her life. It was still hard not to reminisce—any other year she would be celebrating with her parents and friends, not stuck on some island all alone, eating day-old birthday cake while fighting off worries of what might be. Althea was trying hard to care for her, and the officers from the hospital had promised they would make the case their top priority; but after all this time, there still were no answers. Between that and Althea's eerie glances, something felt off, wrong even. Like she wasn't being told the whole truth of some big secret. Her parents were gone, and like her memories, who knew if they would ever return.

Knowing she couldn't deal with that thought now, Ro shifted her focus toward getting more water when the state of the room made her stop. In the brief time she had spent on her phone something had gone amiss. Where the morning sky had been beaming through the windowpanes, all was suddenly dark. One moment, the sun was steadily rising, but now it was gone. Outside, it appeared like the sky was now black, a liquid darkness she had only seen the likeness of in her nightmares.

Walking toward a window, Ro realized that, unlike at night, she couldn't make out anything past her own reflection. The trees, the porch, even the nearby water was all hidden from view, like someone had covered the entire house in a thick, dark cloth. Further away, the harder she looked, it seemed like…

Ro jumped back in alarm as something moved in the distance. There were no other houses on Claudaith Island, and when people came to visit it was normally in the summer. A tall figure moved closer to the house. Someone or something was watching her, and although she couldn't make out any details in the silky void, she felt, much like upstairs, those same eyes peering back at her. With a jolt of fear, Ro rushed to all the windows in the main room, closing the blinds in a flurry.

This had to be a dream. It was simple; she was still in the nightmare—albeit this time it was a slightly different, twisted version. She had simply fallen asleep on the couch, or maybe she had never woken up at all. All Ro had to do was wake up. She squeezed her eyes closed repetitively. It wasn't working. Why couldn't she wake up? Her fear rose and she knew something bad was coming. Feeling as if some invisible entity was closing in around her, the same darkness that always chased her was now advancing in another way. Needing to control the leaping worry and her shaking hands, Ro decided to stay perfectly still, holding her breath.

Maybe, whoever was out there hadn't actually seen her. If it seemed like no one was here then whatever had been staring back would go away. So she stood, shaking in the entrance to the living room. Adrenaline rushed through her as she strained to hear any noises. Though it was oddly quiet, the silence itself seemed as loud as a crowded arena. Ro gripped her cellphone, ready to call for help, but afraid of giving herself away with its light.

That's when she saw it.

Outside, shadows had formed together, squeezing and crawling around both windows before slinking to the door.

A slow, murmured chant encased the house. *"Concede quod petimus, concede quod petimus, concede quod petimus."*

The wind picked up, twisting around the house, and crashing into the door. A loud creak sounded on weathered wood as footsteps landed on the porch.

With wide eyes, Ro watched the shadows cling to one another in front of her, slowly pushing the chain and deadbolt away from its resting position. This had to be another nightmare. She pinched herself a few times, backing away slowly. Multiple footsteps could be heard now. Shivers ran down her spine as a sharp voice pierced through the dark.

"Spaaaarroooow…" The word was long and wispy, both syllables drawn out like they was speaking her name for the first time.

"Spaaaarroooow…"

It's all in my head, she thought, fumbling to call Althea as the sound of that voice sent a chill down her spine. Her eyes didn't leave the looming door as she held the phone to her ear.

A robotic operator informed her she really was alone: *I'm sorry, we are unable to make your call at this time. Please check the number and try your call again.*

Slow creaks and the murmuring voices grew louder. At any moment now, whatever or whomever was outside would enter the house and find her there, terrified and defenceless. Even if this was another nightmare, she had to find a way of escape.

Liquid shadow formations started to pull the door open and Ro ran. With every beat of her pounding heart, she thought of the best places to hide. She was too tall for the kitchen cabinets and to get to her room she would have to go toward the front. Sure, she could always slip out the back, but whatever was trying to get in felt like it was surrounding the house, suffocating it. She rushed into Althea's room in the very back and shut the door behind her.

The bed was too obvious. Didn't most people hide under there in the movies? Her mind raced. Surely the closet and bathroom would be checked if they got in, so the shower was out of the question.

With a bang, the front door swung all the way open, the unlit lamps in the room rattling around her. In between the closet and bathroom doors stood a tall set of wardrobe drawers. Without much time to think, Ro rushed to pull the furniture away from the wall, just enough to squeeze behind. She drew it back toward her, claustrophobically squishing herself against the wall. Ro only hoped the scraping of the dresser against the floorboards hadn't been heard and the fabric draped over the top would shield her from what was to come.

Pounding footsteps erupted throughout the house, a boisterous army storming her home. The shattering of glass and the booms of ransacking reached her ears. They were searching for something. Were they searching for her? Thunder bellowed as lightning spliced the sky. In the momentarily illumination the bedroom door crashed open.

"Sparrow?" The voice was back. "Sparrow, are you in here?"

Ro pushed herself as flat against the back of the

wall as she could, praying to remain unseen.

"We just want to help you, Sparrow, ask a few questions, help you find the truth. But you must come out from hiding."

With slow, deep breaths she forced her body to quit trembling, hoping they couldn't hear her inhaling. As she stood with wide eyes she heard drawers being opened and objects being tossed about.

"I'll check the bathroom," another deep voice said with a gravelly whisper.

Unanswered questions plagued her brain. How did they know her name, and why were they looking for her? None of this made any sense; besides, no one she knew ever called her by her full name.

Her nightmare had never seemed so vivid before. She heard both the bathroom door and the closet being opened on either side of her cramped sanctuary.

The voice continued with a chuckle. "I'm told you prefer to go by Ro?"

A slight breeze hit her as she froze. The shower curtain screeched as it joined the chorus of boxes being torn down from storage.

"Ro, we're here to help."

Breaking in like this was trying to help? Everything felt wrong, the air that surrounded her was heavy with malice. They were crazy. Obviously, this was just a dream, just a dream, just a dream. She repeated the mantra in her head as an old floorboard squeaked close to her right. With eyes closed tight she begged to whatever god there might be to wake her up.

"We're here to help you find your parents, Ro."

Her eyes shot open; this voice she was hearing, these people who had invaded her house and somehow turned the day into night, they knew her parents? They knew where they were? Even though she had every bad feeling about this situation, a strong part of her wanted to leap from behind the dresser and demand answers — to demand to know how they knew who she was. Yet something held her back, some voice deep within her mind, pleading with her to just hold on, to stay hidden.

The voices turned to angry grunts and something smashed close to her.

"She's not in here, boss, we've swept the room clean."

Heavy boots clunked past her and moved further away. She forced herself even tighter against the cool wall.

Click.

Something shifted behind her, air hissing as if released from a soda can, and the room became suffocating. Heavy steps thundered toward her, and Ro braced herself for what was to come. She needed a plan, an idea to defend herself when they finally found her.

Reaching around for anything to wield as a weapon, she grasped an old metal hanger that had been hidden in the dust by her feet. She lifted it in a silent defence when the same slow voice that had been calling out to her spoke again.

"We haven't checked everywhere, have we?"

A silhouette settled to her right.

"Like, say, a ratty old wooden dresser?" The voice shifted into low laughter and the drawers were flung open.

"*Ostendit occultatum*," a dancing voice chimed.

Please don't find me, please just leave, Ro mentally pleaded with the air. She held her breath and braced for an attack.

Though the drawers lay toppled on the ground, it was still pitch black behind the heavy cloth and ornate carvings that shaped the dresser. This was it, either a horrible nightmare she would eventually wake up from, or the strange start to a truly terrifying birthday. She hoped it wouldn't be the latter.

Ro could feel the presence of someone looming over her, a darkened figure biding its time. Slowly, a pale hand wrapped itself around the cloth, fingers intertwined with lace. All they had to do was raise it and reveal her hidden space. There was nowhere left to run, not a single place she could hide. Completely trapped, Ro prepared for the fight.

Then came the scream.

Without the space to cover her ears, she grimaced at the piercing pitch echoing across the house. Someone truly terrified was breaking footsteps from above, sounding as scared as she felt. Ro's heart hammered and she watched the hand whip away. Laughter filled the room once more.

"We found the girl, upstairs now!"

The sound of rushing feet escaped the room as she remembered to breathe. Who was screaming if not her?

That was close. Too close for comfort. She needed to leave. Staying in that tiny space would only get her found once they realized she was not hiding above.

Peeking around the cloth that hung as her shield, Ro examined her limited view of the room. The electricity had not returned, but she could make out the mess. It looked like everyone had left when the scream sounded. Maybe she could find another way to escape while everyone was preoccupied.

Ro tried to shimmy out, only to find she was stuck. It was like something—or someone—had put a heavy weight on top of her, forcing her to remain wedged in that space. Panic set in. Even if this was a dream, she needed to escape. She couldn't be a sitting duck. Her heart rushed to her throat, and she fought to move, but she couldn't.

She was trying to still her staggering panic when a familiar voice interrupted her thoughts. "*Iunctio*. We're on our way, Ro. *Occultatum*. Just stay safe and stay put!"

She was clearly hallucinating things. *Occu*what? *Iuncto*? Those weren't even real words!

The house shook above her as a loud slam echoed against the floors and the walls of the bedroom. Even more reason to escape. She pushed against the furniture as the yelling got louder above her. It felt like the whole house was going to fall to pieces, like she was in the middle of an earthquake. Still, as hard as she fought, she couldn't move very much, and the voice in her head was gone for now. With a few deep breaths she forced herself to relax.

Ro jumped as glass shattered, ringing off nearby surfaces. Realizing the pressure of whatever had been holding her back was gone, she made her way to escape when the dresser suddenly crashed into the trembling floor with a bang.

They had found her. This was it. *At least I might get to know what happened to my mom and dad*, she thought. Fear consumed her as she raised her gaze into the eyes of the one who had torn away her hiding place. Her heart skipped. Ice blue eyes blazed with determination; it was a look she recognized and a face from her past. She clenched the hanger she had grabbed in a petty attempt at defence.

"Sorry, Ro. We've got to leave." His voice sounded tired.

Already unsteady from the roller coaster ripping through her home, Ro teetered as she lost her balance. The wall behind her gave way to an opening. Her eyebrows, once etched with confusion, shot up in shock as his hand flew out to catch her, but it was too late to break her from the fall.

The metal wire she held slipped away like she had slipped from the hand that tried to catch her. The darkness pooled as she flung about for anything to hang onto. Unlike being trapped in her normal nightmare, her stomach dropped and she could feel herself falling rather than being suspended, spiralling into a never-ending abyss.

Something about this felt more real than any dream. The cold air stung as it whooshed past her. She braced herself for what was coming, but this time, unlike her chorus of blood-curdling screams, it was one solid voice, the same one that had found her, crying out one sharp, loud note. "Sparrow!"

CHAPTER TWO

Her forehead was cold. A sticky wet dampness clung to her thundering skull. Wincing, she peeled her eyelids open, dim spots clouding her already compromised vision. Grimacing at newfound aches, she sluggishly noted how still her body was. It was almost peaceful; her previous fear replaced by a calm she hadn't known in a long time. That quickly changed. The cold stone scraped her back and she sat up slowly. Her pounding head screamed against the motion. Ro grimaced as she massaged her neck. A gas lamp swung as someone waved it sporadically, and snippets of conversation reached Ro's ears before she was noticed.

"You think I don't know that?" an annoyed voice chirped. "This tunnel isn't suitable for us to stay in. Its counteractive measure toward those blessed with the power is enough to affect any of us, let alone someone who is untrained and beyond clueless." The voice dropped to a whisper. "Too much time in here and we will be dragging her unresponsive and convulsing body to the surface. Is that what you want?"

"She needs rest," another voice said. "We're lucky there's not even so much as a concussion after that fiasco, and you know the perimeter will be surveyed anyway. Any dampening sickness we can handle now and explain later. I have one objective: to keep you both safe."

A frustrated sigh echoed in the space before they realized Ro watched them, blinking unsteadily.

"Oh, girl! You're awake!"

Thin arms latched around Ro's waist, pulling her to her feet.

"How's the head? You took quite a fall there. Had us worried for a second." The small, pixie-like girl bounced with every word as memories flooded back to Ro. The house, the swishing cloaks, the falling... It hadn't been a dream. She really had fallen into darkness this time. The shock and confusion overwhelmed her and Ro pushed herself away.

"Adyra? What are you doing here?" The gaslight swung violently, casting shadows on darkened walls as she stared at her friend. "Where are we?" The surrounding areas were long and rounded, lit only by the flickering light. It was clear they stood in a dusty, rocky tunnel. "Damping sickness? What's going on?"

Adyra held the lamp in her hand. "I was told you might need help tonight. Where else would I be?" She nudged Ro's shoulder with a quick grin. "Besides, it's been eons since we've seen each other. I missed you, silly." Her bubbly tone did nothing to stop Ro's questions from tumbling out

"You knew I needed help? What do you mean, Adyra?" Unwelcome stress rolled over her. "Adyra you're not making any sense."

"Okay, one question at a time. What's the first thing you want to know?" Adyra's previously genuine smile faltered, no longer fully reaching her eyes.

Ace's voice slid through the shadows. "Sorry to break up the reunion, but we really do have to go. The longer we stay here, the higher our risk of being found." He ran his hand over floppy dark hair with a look that pained Ro. His was a voice she had desperately wanted to hear for months; a voice she had convinced herself she detested; a voice that had abandoned her.

"You want to leave now?" Adyra asked.

"Well, yeah, she's awake now. Come on." His easy smile made Ro wonder if she'd misremembered how he'd told her to leave him alone, erasing years of friendship with a three word text.

No. That had happened. The pain of the rejection was still too fresh to have been imagined. A black pit of anger erupted from deep within her heart and coursed through her shaking body. Was part of her anger misplaced? Possibly, but it had been a rough few months.

Adyra tugged Ro's arm, begging her to join Ace, shooting her a look that screamed, *Chill. It's okay.*

"Answers," Ro demanded. "Now." Her heated face matched her fiery locks.

Adyra's hands shot up in a motion for peace. "Ace is right, we need to get out of here."

"I've got questions," Ro shot out, walking in compliance, her body stiff with anger and confusion.

"You were in trouble," Ace said. "Nice to see you too, Ro"

His sarcastic tone caused her to stop, rolling her eyes as he turned back to look at her. She could tell by the glint in his eye that he was not taking this as seriously as she wanted him to.

"I might not know what's going on here," Ro said. "I might feel nauseous and utterly lost, but one thing I do know is that you lost the right to address me like we're cool. We are not friends anymore, remember? Or did you suddenly forget you wanted nothing to do with me when I left the hospital? What kind of jerkoff does that anyway?"

Ro felt satisfaction at his frustrated sigh.

"Fine, Sparrow," he spit back at her. "We don't have time for this. You want to be angry with me? Sure, be mad. You can channel that anger later okay, but we need to keep walking now"

"Answers first, Aceius," she demanded, planting her feet. "Or I am not going anywhere."

Adyra stepped cautiously into the crossfire. "Ro, he's right," she said softly. "I know you're not happy. I can't even imagine the questions running through your head right now. Well, I can because you asked them, but still… we need to leave." She tugged on Ro's arm. "We can sort out our differences on the way."

Ro glowered but started walking once more, pushing ahead of them.

"We'll answer what we can," Ace said, jogging to come up on her left as Adyra caught up to her right. "And Sparrow," he added with an annoying smirk, "you can still call me Ace."

Light bounced off one dirt wall to the next. Ro took a deep breath, momentarily breaking her irritation. She would be the bigger person in this; she would swallow her anger if it helped her get to the truth. Right now, she just needed clarity. "You said I needed help?" she asked, turning to Adrya.

The short girl giggled. "Well, your house was under attack and you had to hide from creepy hooded people. I would call that needing help. We knew you were going to need a safe way out of there."

"Yes, but how did you know?" Ro's headache raged, but she was determined to keep pushing.

Ace cut in. "Althea told us."

"Yep, Althea called, so here we are!"

"That doesn't answer anything!" Ro said, panting. "Neither of you are that close with Althea. She wasn't even home."

Adyra fidgeted a little and handed the lamp to Ace. "Let's just say there is a system in order to help you if the need arises. Like a phone tree. Ace and I are on the list. Besides, it's a good thing that we were there or else you wouldn't have found a way off Claudaith."

Ro shot them both a look of indignation. "Okay, so ignoring the fact that you are hiding something from me, I'll indulge you. Are we not still on Claudaith? How did we even get here? The last thing I remember is falling."

"Oh, you fell alright," Adyra confirmed. "After I created the diversion—thanks for making it difficult by the way by trying to get up and leave when we were clearly coming to get you. Ace here wouldn't stop going on about how you were 'breaking the bind and attempting to escape without us.'" Adyra mimicked his deeper tone as she said quoted him. "So, I remained stationed while he went to where you were hiding."

"Wait..." Sparrow said as recollection of those last moments behind the dresser flooded back. "I knew I could hear your voice; how did you do that?" She jabbed her finger at him and turned fully as he batted it away, walking backwards so she could stare at his face.

"The bind or the message?" he asked. "Either way, I can't tell you, it's a secret, and I'm not quite ready to break any laws yet." He winked with a tilt of his head. "Anyway, by the time I got there, you must've unlocked the false back and were already falling in."

"What laws?" Sparrow huffed.

"Laws that stop Adyra or me from telling you too much until we know you are out of harm's way," he muttered.

Ro's stomach roiled. "False back?" she asked. A wave of nausea threatened to overcome her, and she closed her eyes to push it down again. She turned back around. Their pace was intense, the ground more uneven while increasingly uphill.

"Yes, a false back. Behind the dresser was an entry to the tunnel we're in now." Ace grabbed her arm as she swayed a bit. "Are you okay?"

"I'm fine!" She jerked away, fighting not to focus on the dots threatening to cover her vision.

Adyra gently grabbed her other arm in support as Ace looked on in concern.

"We need to get you out of here," he mumbled, turning to Adyra. "I told you the charm wouldn't last for long."

"Don't look at me," Adyra said. "Althea's the one who made it. Isn't medicine supposed to be like, her thing or something?"

Ro felt Adyra place a hand on her clammy back. "It's just the tunnel, sweetie, it has this effect on people who seldom travel it. Don't worry. As soon as we reach fresh air, you'll feel better."

"I'm fine." Ro swallowed thickly, determined to push on. Her body felt numb as her heavy feet continued their trek. "You said tunnel? On Claudaith?"

"You must have somehow opened the hatch that locked the entryway to the tunnels," Adyra answered over Ace's concerned grumbles

"I tried to catch you," Ace offered.

"Yes, yes," Adyra continued, her voice calm. "He did try, but you had already fallen to the ground of the tunnel. Ace raced down right away to make sure you were okay; I created another diversion until we could sneak away."

Ro looked to Ace sharply. "But my head? I remember striking something hard and it felt like I fell into a nightmare."

"You were knocked unconscious, but otherwise you were okay. I made sure of it before we got you mostly through the tunnel."

"Mostly? I thought the only way off the island was by the ferry?"

"It is," Adyra continued. "Unless you know of this path. Althea wanted it kept a secret, only to be used when necessary. The tunnel runs underground, leading from the house to Aylee."

Ro looked at her in shock "Aylee? That's on the mainland! That means that this tunnel would have to run under the ocean." The small, cramped space they walked through suddenly felt like it was going to suffocate her. Her eyes swam as the nausea increased again.

"It's fine,"Adyra assured her, but her voice was laced with concern as she looked to Ace for help.

"She's right," Ace said. "The tunnel runs 700 feet underground, but if it helps you feel better, we are almost to the surface. We should be there any minute now." His analytical tone was oddly reassuring as Ro's stomach turned in protest once more.

"Okay." She breathed deeply, pacing out her words thickly. "So you're telling me we are in a tunnel that stretches under the island to the mainland, and that Althea sent you to help me?"

At this point, both Ace and Adyra were supporting her as they moved forward. Ro didn't care enough to shrug them off. "This doesn't make any sense," she said. "Who were those people who trashed the house? Why were they looking for me?"

The air became lighter and the flame in the lantern flickered as a cool breeze whistled through the tunnel. "It will make sense eventually," Adyra said, the note of a giggle on her voice like someone holding a secret. "If I told you now, you wouldn't believe me."

"At least tell me why they were after me. That guy said… he said he knew about my parents." Exasperation leaked into her tone as they came to a sudden stop. She turned to look at her friend.

"They are called the Nef—" Adyra began, but she was rudely interrupted.

"We're here!" Ace called out.

A short ladder stood in front of them, leading up to a rusted hatch. "I'll go first, just to make sure it's safe," Ace said as he stepped onto the first rung, smirking at Ro as she asked, "Safe from what?"

Daylight flooded the dust-ridden area when Ace reached the hatch, specks danced in their eyes as Ro's pupils struggled to adjust.

"Do you feel well enough to climb up?" Adyra extinguished the lantern and placed it along the wall, concern in her voice.

"Yeah," Ro said. "I'm actually feeling a bit better."

And she was, with the sudden opening to the outside world Ro noticed the heaviness drifting away and the nausea dissipating.

"See, I told you once we reached the surface you

would be alright. This tunnel has a way of making some of us a bit sick."

Adyra smiled as Ro grabbed onto the ladder and started to climb. With every step up her strength increased, and her headache disappeared.

As she stepped out of the shaft, she grabbed onto Ace's hand for support. She felt herself lose her balance and fell toward him. She found her footing, and when she looked up, she realized she was close enough to see the green specks in his eyes.

"You okay?" he asked with a smile.

She jerked herself a safe distance away.

"Yes, fine…"

You can be nicer than that, her guilt screamed at her. "Thank you… I mean we are far from okay, but thank you for helping me."

"Anytime, Ro," he said.

"Ready to go?" Adyra said, emerging from the tunnel shaft.

"I'm still expecting answers, you jerk!" Ro called after Ace's retreating form as he continued forward, expecting them to follow.

Ro surveyed her surroundings. They were completely surrounded by trees, and a few rusty cars sat on the windblown ground. "This is Aylee?" she wondered aloud

"Not exactly," her bubbly friend said. "We're right outside though. This land has been abandoned for a few years now. We keep a car here for emergencies."

"We? You make it sound like you're a part of some

team or something," Ro said.

Adyra shrugged, refusing to look Ro in the face "There's a lot you don't know yet."

"Then tell me," Ro demanded. She was tired of having no answers. The darkness that had crept into her house had left her afraid. Right now though, she felt more annoyed than anything. She deserved answers; she needed to know.

Adyra only gestured ahead, ignoring questions. "Come on, let's get in."

A rusty black car sat before them, covered in dirt. It sputtered to a start as Ro climbed into the back.

"Why can't you just tell me now?" She grabbed the edges of the seat as the car bounced down a dirt road.

Ace's brows quirked, meeting hers in the rearview mirror. "I thought you would be happy to see us after such a long time. Haven't you heard of curiosity killing the cat?"

"Ace!" Adyra lightly smacked his shoulder. "She's not a cat. You would have questions too." She turned to face Ro. "Just trust me as your friend to tell you when I can, okay?"

Her pleading brown eyes caught in the sunlight and Ro sighed in partial defeat. "Will you at least tell me where we're going?"

"Tonight, we are staying in Aylee."

"That's not what I meant. Long term, what's the plan?"

"We *are* actually staying in Aylee," Ace insisted. "It's far enough away from the coast that no one will suspect we are there, and it's so late we can get some rest and get an early start in the morning."

"Like the people who broke into my house? They're still looking for me?"

"Yes," Adyra replied hesitantly.

"So, if they are looking for me, then they could be anywhere. How do I know I can trust *you*? I've got no information, and globs of black ink and weird hooded guys just attacked me with spells or charms or something."

Ace rolled his eyes at her in the mirror. "Ro, I need you to stop pushing on things we can't tell you yet."

"Yeah, well, you're a plebe," she shot back.

"We have known each other since birth. Our parents are close, and Adyra has been your best friend since the fifth grade. I know you're frustrated because we can't give you all the answers you want right now, but do you really think we would hurt you, and on your birthday?"

Adyra's chin rested on the back of the bench seat, her face a wash of hurt and concern that filled Ro with guilt.

"No," she mumbled. "I know I can trust at least one of you."

"Really, this again?" Ace looked to Adyra for help, but she only offered a small smile.

"What do you mean, again?" Ro glared at the back of his head. "We haven't even talked about it! Not that you could have any excuse at all for what you did…"

"What *I* did? I protected you, Sparrow; we saved

you." His voice clipped out at her through clenched teeth. "And correct me if I'm wrong, but we're *still* in the process of saving you. Just let bygones be bygones!"

"Bygones? Do you even know what that word means?"

"You have no clue how hard it's been, not being allowed to let you—"

"Enough!" Adyra interrupted briskly, her long brown hair whipped into a frenzy. "We are all tired, we are all stressed. It has been a long and emotional day. Ro, you are confused and still mad at Ace. Ace, you haven't slept in three days and could get in serious trouble if you keep talking. Just shut up and enjoy the ride will you! I don't want to be stuck in this car with the both of you bickering!" Annoyance had caused her face to flush, turning her freckles red.

"Fine!" Ro and Ace said in unison, glaring.

At least the seat is comfortable, Ro thought as she slumped against it in silence.

The sky turned to twilight as they entered the small town of Aylee. Surrounded by trees and a few yellow streetlights, gas stations and corner shops littered the sides of the badly paved road. Several cars travelled past as the song of the cicadas floated through the open windows, interrupting the tense silence within the vehicle. A green, sun-worn interstate sign caught her eye as she looked up to see the headlights of cars exiting and entering Aylee. It seemed like another small boring town; the saving grace being the fact that the coast was only an hour away. *Well,* Ro thought, *better this one stop truck stop boom town than the remains of the old cottage I woke up in this morning.*

Deep in thought, Ro didn't notice when they turned to the left of the interstate toward a small motel. Although she had no clue what the future held, she did feel bad for upsetting Adyra. And as angry as she was with Ace, he did look exhausted. Ro took this moment to really examine her companions. Puffy bags the colour of a bruise hung under Ace's eyes, and his normally tan complexion was washed with grey. Adyra didn't look as worn, but just as stressed, her hair messy and her face pale. Whatever they weren't telling her was bad.

A sudden stop jolted her forward, and she watched as Ace left the car. "What next?" she groaned, cracking her back as she sat up straight.

"Ace will check us in and pick up dinner from the diner across the street. Come on, let's get the bags."

"Bags?"

She followed Adyra around to the open trunk where two black duffels sat.

"Yep," Adyra said. "Althea stashed some supplies and clothes after you moved in."

"So, she knew we would be travelling?"

"Not exactly. It was always option B, you know?"

They each grabbed a bag and hoisted it over their shoulders as Ace came back and tossed them a key.

"Which room?" Adyra called.

"22B."

She sighed and gave Ro a look of hesitation. "Come on. I don't know about you, but I could kill for a shower."

"Agreed, I could eat as well." Ro smiled in response, but it felt forced.

The room was small, tiny even, with two beds, matching bedside tables, and a small TV.

"Sorry it's not much," Adyra said. "But it's the best we could find this close to the interstate." She dropped her bag on the floor.

"It's fine. It has a bed and that's all that matters."

"True. Your clothes should be in the one you're holding if you want to shower first. It might take Ace a minute to get the food."

Ro crouched down, unzipping the bag to find some clean clothes. A medical kit flopped onto the white tiled floor revealing a stack of cash that had been hidden underneath. "Listen," she said, looking up at Adyra. "I'm sorry I made you angry. This is all just so…"

"Frustrating and confusing? I know." Adyra smiled. "I wish I could give you the answers you need, but I can't."

"Can you at least tell me what I saw? I mean inky shadows opening doors, that's… impossible, right?"

"It's not safe to talk about it. We must follow protocol. I'm not saying you're wrong or crazy, but I can't give you any details." Adyra sighed. "We will tell you everything as soon as we get you out of here."

"Safe from… those people?"

"Yes, in short, as soon as we are far enough away from Claudaith, you will know, okay?"

An embarrassing rumble caused Ro to jump.

Adyra laughed. "Your stomach sounds like it's trying to eat itself."

"Yeah, I guess I haven't eaten anything today."

"Well, that's not right for your 19th. Maybe Ace will bring back some cake or something."

"At this point, any food will do."

"I am really glad to see you, Ro," Adyra said.

Ro smiled. "So, what's in the other duffel?" she asked.

"Oh, just some more clothes and supplies."

"For you and Ace?"

Adyra got up quickly, moving to arrange the pullout couch.

"Yeah, uh, I've got clothes in there for tomorrow."

"Oh, so we're going somewhere close by then?" It was so quiet Ro could have sworn she heard crickets. "Adyra?"

"So, I figure I will take one bed and you can have the other. Ace can sleep on the pullout." She lined the mattress with a top sheet.

"What are you avoiding?" Ro asked.

With a defeated sigh, the small girl sat down to face her. She looked tired beyond her years.

"I didn't want to tell you yet because I know you're upset with how Ace ended your friendship. And you were just attacked, so that warrants some anxiety, but I won't be going with you tomorrow. I'm leaving earlier, before you wake up."

"But that's —"

"Not fair? I know. Ace and I have differing jobs in this. He can get you to the meetup point safely. I have a lead on someone who can help us that was close to your family. I know you want to protest this, I do, but besides this being our job, you're our friend. This is the best-case scenario."

Tiredness began to creep behind Ro's eyes again. "Your job? The only job you have ever had was the haunted house last year! If you fill me in on what's going on then maybe I could keep myself safe!"

"Ro, this goes a lot deeper than you know. It's not —"

"Safe? I get it!" Ro looked up, seeking patience from the motel ceiling. "You're going to talk to someone I know? Someone close to my family?" She spoke slowly, an idea forming.

"Yes, someone who can give us more information on your attack."

With a deep breath and facing the facts, Ro knew two things: something abnormal was happening around her, and someone close to her family might be able to help. Yes, she hated to think that Adyra and Ace weren't actually helping her, but who could she trust? Back on Claudaith it appeared that those shadows defied the laws of physics, being manipulated with words like a spell or something. That's why she had been so convinced it was a dream. None of this felt right. Even talking with Adyra, something felt off.

How can I trust and travel with people who are obviously

keeping something from me? she thought. It was clear they weren't going to give her any answers until they were ready, and normally she would have respected that, but right now she didn't know who to trust. The cloaked figures… they had mentioned her parents. They had information about what happened to them.

Of course, she couldn't trust that slimy voice at all. If someone is on your side they don't attack your home, but if all they needed was someone that could help her, who not only knew her parents but was trustworthy, then she might just know the perfect person. Ro highly doubted Ace and Adyra would just come around to her way of thinking though, and that could be a problem.

"Girl, you okay?" Adyra asked.

Ro shook herself from her stupor.

"Yeah. If you say that travelling with Ace is the best plan while you find this person, then okay. I trust you." She dialled her smile up to a ten and gave a reassuring nod.

"Thank you! I was so worried about telling you because I know that you and Ace are fighting right now — well *you're* fighting with him — but thank you for trusting me!"

Adyra pulled her into a tight embrace.

Guilt was going to make her spill if she didn't put her plan into motion, Ro just knew it. She pulled quickly away from the hug. Ace and Adyra weren't bad people and she really didn't like deceiving them. "Alright well, I am going to take a shower, it's been a nightmare of a day, literally."

She grabbed the clothes from the duffle bag, palming some of the cash at the same time, and headed toward the dingy bathroom.

"Sure!" Adyra called out. "I'll let you know when the food is here."

Before her conscience forced her to reveal her plan, Ro shut the door on her companion.

With a twist, she collapsed against the sink, letting out a stressed sigh. *It wasn't really a lie if it helped out right?* Ro turned on the water in the tub and looked at herself in the foggy bathroom mirror as the shower droned on in the background. Pulling her hair into a messy ponytail and wiping yesterday's mascara from under her eyes, she looked around for a way to escape. It wasn't that she didn't trust her companions, and she was grateful to them for getting her out of whatever hellish situation this morning had been, but she could not blindly follow them to some random place just because they told her it was safe. She might consider that option if she had no plan that was better, but Adyra had given her another idea.

A rusted window frame was just above her eye-line. Sure, it wasn't an amazing idea, but she should be able to slide through it. Beggars can't be choosers, right? Ditching the dirty clothes for the jeans and a sweater that had been in the duffel, Ro dressed quickly then pushed her phone and the cash into her pocket before carefully climbing to the top of the toilet. With both hands against the window, she pushed it along its metal track, wincing as it slid with a whine. Clicking it into place, Ro jumped, gripping the ledge for balance. She could hear the TV in the main room. The coast seemed to be clear. Breathing a sigh of relief, Ro pulled herself through the window.

The moon illuminated the grass as she crashed into the ground. Twigs and a bush broke her fall and she fought to keep in a groan of pain. Standing on sore legs, Ro peered up to the window, worried that her escape might have been foiled by the noise. All she could hear was the shower running and faint laughter coming from the television. Turning around in the dark, she realized how lucky it was that they had gotten a side room. Had they been in the front of the building someone would have certainly seen her slip out to run away. Taking a reassuring breath, she bolted across the empty lot toward a brightly lit gas station. It became her goal, her hopeful sanctuary. Wide-eyed and gasping for air, Ro knew she needed to hurry. When they realized she wasn't in the shower, let alone in the motel room, they would come looking for her. She didn't know how much time she had.

She sputtered against her hair as it whipped about wildly. *Just get to the station,* she thought. *One step at a time.*

Ro knew she had to figure this out on her own, she had to learn the truth. The unnatural darkness that had surrounded Althea's house, the people who had chased her, Ace's voice in her mind… these things weren't normal, none of this was normal. People she thought she could trust, friends she had known for most of her life, that she had felt an unbreakable bond with yet hadn't spoken to since that horrible day, were suddenly appearing in her world—providing no answers to the burning questions she had and asking her to trust them when they had disappeared the moment she needed them most. *I'm done being scared and confused,* Ro told herself, almost to her destination now. Besides, if someone was really after her, then she was putting both Ace and Adyra at risk the longer they stayed together.

Any second now they could discover she was gone, so the more distance she put between her and that cramped motel room the better. Foggy lights illuminated the ground as she finally made it to the gas station and slowed to a walk. Attempting to look as normal as possible, Ro searched for a way out of Aylee. Once she was far enough away, she would find a ride to her next destination, but right now, her first focus was getting enough space between her and that ratty motel as possible.

A sputtering old Ford sat alone at the pumps, its owners inside the station. Looking around to ensure no one could see her, Ro quickly lifted herself over the tailgate and lay as flat as possible against the rubble in the back. The cold, ridged metal pressed against her, and she pulled the tarp over herself to hide.

Straining, she could hear two voices approaching. With a jolt of weight, the old truck adjusted, rumbling to life, getting ready to leave with her on board this chariot of escape.

All she had to do was stay hidden until the next stop. Getting as far away as she could, though hopefully closer to the destination she had in mind: to someone she knew she could trust to give her the answers she needed, someone who had always been there for her.

The florescent lights faded away as stars flooded her vision. A few strands of hair shot out from the hold she had wrapped them in, racing with the roaring wind as they turned onto a busier highway, but that didn't bother her.

One thought pierced her mind as her eyes got heavier: *It was all going to be okay. It had to be.*

CHAPTER THREE

The thorny bush scratched at her sides. Nearby, the slow crawl of a river trickling over smooth rocks echoed around two figures in the clearing directly in front of her. Ro sat quietly, mesmerized by the scene ahead, locked in a daze. Two figures draped in heavy, flowing cloaks, were in conversation, their faces hidden by hoods jutting into a V covering their faces, and falling to a sharp point just past their noses. They stood as stark silhouettes against the bright moon.

"Something feels wrong," Ro thought. Like the world was slightly tilted on its axis. She shivered in the chilly air. There was no wind. A bad taste flooded Ro's mouth, reminding her of the natto she had once dared to eat, but this taste had a stench, one much worse than fermented soybeans. If one could feast on vileness, she was sure it would have a tang like this. Ro grimaced as she focused ahead.

Two low voices growled in the darkness.

"Gone," one said. "They got to her before we did."

"How? There's only one way off that island. Have your men scoured every inch?"

"Not an option. We had to fall back on the risk of being found. You know we cannot be caught. Discretion is our most important weapon."

"They're not going to be happy, and what of Olrod?"

"The mole? He was discovered, held by the court now. He's requesting our assistance."

"He's a spineless prat who ratted out his own; besides, he doesn't even know who any of us really are. The girl is our main concern now. We cannot report this back yet, they won't accept failure."

"We still have a chance; patience is a virtue. The girl is smart, but she's clueless to who she really is. We have eyes looking now, and trip spells for any barrier."

The wind started suddenly, biting through the trees, and ruffling the shadowed figures who grew louder and angrier by the minute. Yet it was harder to concentrate on what they were saying.

Why was it suddenly so warm? Ro wondered, glancing down at her reddening skin. It was an endlessly cold, dark night; yet she could no longer feel the frigid air or the jabbing twigs she crouched upon. Ro shook the pressure from her head as fog crept along her vision. She could hear her own heartbeat as her pulse increased. I'm so tired, Ro thought, as she fought to focus on the conversation between the two parties. Something told her it was important to stay there, stay in the moment. Still, she felt herself slipping, falling away. Though fighting against collapsing back, she felt her body give into the fog.

Up ahead, one last sentence pierced her mind as the darkness took over again. "The Nefarie will rise."

A jostling stop shook her to consciousness and Ro found herself blinking at a vivid blue sky that glared back at her, the tarp having fallen off as she slept. Two doors opened and the truck adjusted to the missing weight of its drivers as the doors slammed. Slipping out from her hiding spot, Ro thought back to her weird dream. She couldn't shake the feeling that she had witnessed something important. It had been oddly lifelike, remains of the nasty taste still clinging to her tongue.

Shaking the night away, Ro hoped the coast was clear. Rising to peer over the edge of the truck, she realized they had parked in the lot of a grocery store. The sound of buggies being pushed joined the chorus of birds chirping as the breeze ruffled the leaves of a nearby tree. Quickly jumping to the ground, Ro looked for any clear sign of where she could be. *Hopefully I've gone far enough*, she thought while stretching.

Even though they had driven through the night, it might not have been enough distance between her and her old friends. Ro bit her lip as a mix of guilt and worry washed over her; they would know she was gone by now.

Smoothing her tangled mess of hair, Ro walked toward the shops along the street. Most of them were closed, many signs stating opening times of 10 a.m., so it must have still been early. Catching her ragged appearance in a window, Ro quickly straightened her crumpled outfit. She looked tired, stressed, and worried. "Oh god," Ro muttered. "How am I going to get anywhere without a plan?" And now she was the funny girl talking to a reflection… great. "Ugh, alright, Sparrow. Get it together. First find out where you are then figure out transportation, easy peasy."

Hoping no one saw her momentary lapse of sanity, Ro took a deep breath and turned to go. Her stomach roared in protest, reminding her she still hadn't eaten.

Okay. Step one: get food. Step two: find out where you are.

She walked toward the smell of freshly baked bread.

A small bakery sat off a side street, begging her to come in. Her mouth watered at the idea of all the yummy pastries calling to her from inside. She slowly entered, hoping not to seem too eager for food.

"Hi, how can I help you?" A younger man smiled at her from behind the counter.

Overwhelmed by options, Ro let the first thing she thought of slip from her mind.

"A cinnamon roll and some water?"

"Sure." He grinned as tatted arms typed on the tablet in front of him. "That'll be $9.45."

Pulling out the jumbled wad of cash, Ro hoped she appeared natural. She smiled as he printed her receipt. Ro dropped her change into the tip jar as he put the pastry in a bag for her. Since it was slow and there was no line, she decided to take a risk. "Can I ask you something?"

His head tilted in curiosity as he passed her the bag. "Sure, what's up?"

She laughed awkwardly. "I was wondering if you

could tell me how far Peates Cove is from here? I'm a bit directionally challenged and" —Ro held up her phone— "unfortunately my phone chose this moment to go kaput, or I'd look it up myself."

"Oh, sure," he said. "That's like thirty minutes by car. Are you heading that way or…?" The question trailed off and he seemed to catch himself. "I mean, we don't get too many visitors here unless they're just passing through? Small town and all."

"Yeah, actually, I have an uncle who lives there, and I think I got off the bus too early."

"The directionally challenged thing again?" he asked, laughing.

"Yeah, that and I was really craving a cinnamon roll." She lifted the bag.

"Well, I'm sure he will be happy to see you," he replied with a kind smile.

"Yeah, um, would you by chance have a phone here I could use? Just so I could call a taxi for the rest of the way? And call to let him know I'm safe, of course." Ro couldn't believe how lucky she was that Peates Cove was close to where she wound up.

"Sure! Do you need a number for a cab company or…?"

"That would be great since as I can't look it up." She grinned as he walked away.

The pastry was warm and sweet, crumbling as she pulled it apart. It was all Ro could do not to inhale the whole thing in one bite.

"Here you go."

She jumped as an outstretched hand held an old black house phone to her.

"Thanks!" She brushed the crumbs of her breakfast away as she took it.

"No problem. I also wrote down the closest cab company's number." He set down a crumpled note with her water.

She smiled and waited until he was a safe distance away to call. She needed to get out of there. Ro knew her story wasn't a great one; heck, she was surprised the cashier believed her in the first place. She didn't even believe herself. It wouldn't be long before Adyra was hot on her trail. She only hoped dialling 0 would still help her find a number.

A woman's voice cut through the line. "Operator speaking, how can I help you?"

"I'm looking for an address."

"What's the name and area?"

"Pericuios Smith. He lives in Peates Cove."

The distinct sound of typing filled the speaker before the woman's bland voice chimed back in. "I have one Pericuios Smith in Peates Cove. Did you want the address?"

"Yes, please," Ro said as she wrote down the response and hung up.

No one had entered the small shop and the person who had taken her order was nowhere to be found as she quickly arranged for a cab and left the phone on the counter on her way out.

Walking to an old bench, she let the sun warm her

skin as she took a few calming breaths. It had been a long two days and she could almost feel herself slip away into the land of dreams. The peaceful smell of salt water filled her lungs as she did her best to push the anxiety down.

"Order a ride, hunny?" an older woman's voice called.

Opening her eyes, Ro saw an old, battered cab had pulled up in front of her.

"Yes, ma'am." She smiled and the woman grinned back.

"Well, get in then, we don't have all day." Though the words were abrupt, her voice was filled with kindness.

Ro opened the cab's back door and strapped herself into the seat. "Thank you!"

"No problem, dear!" The car jolted forward, slowly rolling away from the curb.

"We're going to 1836 E Capers in Peates Cove, right?"

"Yes, ma'am."

"Such a long way for one person to go alone." Curious eyes met Ro's gaze and she felt her defences rise. If this lady suspected anything, all her plans could go awry.

Oh, you know, Ro thought. *I'm just going to visit my godfather whom I haven't seen in years to hope that he can tell me why shadow people are after me. Oh, and I left the two people who rescued me in some crappy motel a couple of hours back. You know, the usual!* Ro was sure that response would end with her being committed. She offered all the fake enthusiasm she could muster and answered simply, "I'm going to see my uncle."

"That's nice. I can never get my grandkids to visit anymore, least of all my nieces." The lady chuckled as they left the small town and turned onto an old tree lined highway.

"Yeah, my parents sent me to visit for a while."

"For the holidays? Do you have lots of plans?"

Ro stiffened in her seat. "I'm really not sure. I guess we are just taking it as it comes."

Sharp eyes met hers in the rearview mirror, arched in unbelief. "Kind of strange that you're not spending your holidays with your parents then?"

Panic rose to her throat. Could this lady tell she was lying, was she that easy to see through? "Not really... I used to spend holidays there, but haven't the past few years." Ro averted her eyes to the tinted windows. Silence settled over them as the cab rambled on, finally passing a sign for the small community her godfather lived in.

Her thoughts drifted to the companions she left behind. Would they be looking for her? Did Adyra still go to meet with whoever? What about the people who were after them, could they be tracking her still too? Thoughts of the moment when the safe warmth of Althea's house had been shattered hung heavily around her. Hiding behind that dresser, thinking she was going to be found. What if they suddenly showed up again? Could this all be connected to the disappearance of her parents? She wouldn't have been at Althea's if they hadn't gone missing. Should she try to contact the investigating officer? Did their disappearance have something to do with the people who were after her, with why Ace and Adyra were acting so weird? Ro knew last night's dream had been nothing like her normal night terrors, but what about tonight? Worries filled her mind as the cab turned onto an old road lined with big silver gates, each about a mile apart.

They slowed to a stop, the lady's voice interrupting Ro's anxiety. "We're here, dear"

"How much do I owe you?" Ro unbuckled the seatbelt and leaned toward the woman.

"$87.95."

She counted out the money and handed it over with a rush.

"Sorry for all the questions," the woman said. "It's just the people who live in this community are more secluded and keep to themselves more than most." Her smile was kind again as Ro closed the cab door.

"Have a good holiday!" the woman called out her open window.

"Thanks. You too."

The cab rolled back into the road, carting the inquisitive old woman with it.

Taking a deep breath for reassurance, Ro faced the property in front of her. A silver gate towered high above the driveway set behind it. There was no call box, no mailbox, no way to contact the owners of this extravagant entrance. She could just slip in and walk to the house. If this were Peri's house, he would be happy to see her, right? If it weren't she would not only be trespassing on a stranger's land, but she would be at another dead end. *Where could I go from there?* Ro wondered. Time was ticking, and she had already come this far. *What's the worst that could happen?* Determined, she slipped through the main gate and quickly walked up the hill. *Why does anyone need a driveway this long?* Soon enough, a large wooden house came into view, almost cabin- like. The sun glistened off the gold-tinged door.

Swallowing her doubt, Ro jogged up the steps. She hoped that Peri would take her in and explain everything in a way that only an adult could and tell her it was all going to be okay. No matter how much time had passed, he was her godfather, her dad's best friend, and nothing was more important than family. Forming a shaky fist, she knocked, the stained-glass window of the door vibrating slightly with each rap. Not a second later it opened with a force, causing her to jump back.

Surprise and curiosity filled her as she looked up into the tired and hardened face of the man who stood in front of her. A simple suit and tie matched his groomed physique but not his exhausted and shocked expression as he stared back down at her.

"Sparrow...?" he questioned.

"Hi, Peri." She shot him a watery smile. All the pain and fear she had been holding in broke past the dam she had locked them behind. At the sight of her family, someone she loved and could trust, her guard broke down. She rushed in, hugging him, choking back her tears as she focused on the fact that she had succeeded.

Offering a reassuring smile, he pulled away. "Ro, where have you been? We've been worried sick."

"We?" Ro sniffled.

"Althea contacted me when you ran from Adyra and Ace. She's been freaking out! I know I always told you to rebel, but really, Ro? Your godmother can't handle a heart attack." He stood aside. "Well, come in. My home is yours. You know that."

"Althea contacted you?" Ro gaped. "But she hates you."

"She might dislike me, but she loves you. You know how she is, a worry-wart."

They sat on a nearby couch.

"Peri, what's going on?" Ro asked.

"Well, you're going to explain yourself, and after this chat, I'm going to ring Althea so she knows you're okay."

She grimaced. "I came here for answers. The fact that you knew I was with Adyra and Ace means you know something. So, spill."

He sighed, the tired expression creeping back into his eyes.

"Well, Ro, what do you already know?"

She leaned back, sinking into the leather.

"Well, I've been staying with Althea."

"I know."

"So, you know about my parents then." It wasn't a question.

He offered an apologetic look before continuing.

"The authorities contacted both Althea and me. I know what it must have seemed like — me not reaching out to you — but since the divorce was finalized I must say I've been quite the chicken about talking with her again. I hope you can forgive me." The smile dropped and he looked like a regretful, middle-aged man.

Ro swallowed her tears and pushed through. "I know. I mean, I figured. The point is, you're here for me now right, and I need your help, Peri."

"I'll tell you what I know, everything, but first tell me what happened at Althea's."

Ro spilled everything that had occurred in the past twenty-four hours. From the attack at the house — he was mad at that — to running away and calling a cab.

He looked a little impressed, and a smile graced his lips, brightening his face. "Well, if anything, at least you're resourceful." Peri laughed before spreading his arms in a gesture of transparency. "What do you want to know? I will try to answer as best I can."

Someone was finally going to tell her the truth. Confident in her decision to turn to her family, she unleashed her questions. "Who is after me?"

"You think they are still after you?"

"I mean, who destroyed Althea's house? Adyra said they were after me."

"Ro, there are things you don't know about this world."

"Spare me the 'you're a kid and I'm an adult' rant." Her words contained a biting snark. "You don't have to protect me. I am 19 now."

He raised his hands in defence. "That's why this started. It's because you are 19. There is a small group who think you now have the means to help them."

"Help them?"

"Yes. You and your family."

"Wouldn't that put you in danger too?"

"No We are not blood related, so I can't help them. But that doesn't mean you're not family, Ro. I'll make sure they can't harm you here."

"Can't we just go to the police or something? There's a detective on Mom and Dad's case, I'm sure he can help."

"No," he barked. "Ro, they won't understand. The best way to keep you safe is to keep others out of it. They already have your mom and dad."

She stared in shock. "My parents? So these people are the reason they are..."

"Missing? Yes." His face was pained. "The point is, if we want to find them, we can't go to the police, okay?"

"So, you can find them? You know where they are?" Hope filled her for the first time in what felt like forever.

"I don't know for sure, but I have an idea." He smiled at her. "We will get them back."

Get them back; the words resounded in her mind. She would be with her family once again. Everything would be okay. There was just one problem.

"What about Ace and Adyra? They must be looking for me by now."

"Oh, they are," Annoyance graced his aging features. "I told them not to send such young and irresponsible—"

"They saved me, remember?" she cut into his rant. "If it wasn't for them, I might not have made it here. And who sent them?"

"I'm happy they got you out of there," Peri said. "The Nefarie are not to be taken lightly. I have some friends in high places who are looking after your—our—family."

"Nefarie?" she questioned. "Friends?"

"Yes," Peri responded, ignoring her first question and diving right into the second. "Friends. A group of us feared this day might come, Althea included Aceius' and Adyra's families when you were young."

"You haven't been around much since the divorce… why would she include you?" Ro asked in confusion.

"Well, we all bound together for the greater good," he said, standing up. "Besides, she was always more in love with her plants than me."

He wasn't wrong, she would spend hours in her greenhouse, catering to the plant's needs. Reading, talking, and playing music to the many varieties she had collected throughout the years.

Be the bigger person during petty drama, Ro told herself.

Her godparent's relationship had always been a petty one. Althea setting the thermostat to a freezing temperature when Peri wasn't looking, him always getting her back by turning off her watering systems for the plants whenever she left the house. But she had bigger fish to fry. "Wait," she said. "I still don't understand. Who are these friends?"

"Some of them are coming over in about an hour. Why don't you head upstairs? The guest bedroom is on the right, and later you can meet them to get more answers." He walked her to the foot of the nearby staircase.

"You said you would tell me!" she protested.

"And I will, but you're going to want to meet them to fully understand. Besides, I must let Althea know you're okay."

Guilt washed over her at the thought of the older woman wringing her hands with worry.

"Okay," Ro conceded. It wasn't the worst situation. At least he'd given her a name for the cloaked figures. *Nefarie*. It was the same title she'd heard in her dreams.

"Good," Peri said. "Get some rest and I'll let you know when they're here. You've got to be bone tired, love."

Ro had just turned to go up to the guest room when he called out once more. "Sparrow," he said. "I really am glad you're here and safe. I hope you know that I've only ever wanted what's best for you." "

"Thanks, Peri." She smiled and reached in for another hug.

Suddenly, there was an agonizing burn on her wrist, searing into her flesh and causing her to cry out.

"What the?!" She jerked away, the pain travelling up her right arm. A quick glance at her wrist showed her silver bracelet flashing red with an angry heat.

"Are you okay?" Peri asked, face crumpled in concern.

"Yes, it's just uh…" She trailed off, unsure how to explain. "When my arm touched yours, it sounds stupid, but I could have sworn my bracelet burned me."

"Your bracelet?" He looked down to the wispy chain that circled her wrist, twisted into various rose petals of a similar design trailing along the chain as if they were on a vine. "Yeah, it's like it scalded me. I swear it glowed, but now it's fine." She looked at it curiously, now cool to the touch.

"You have your mom's' bracelet," he muttered strangely.

"She gave it to me before she, the day before she…" Ro couldn't seem to get out the words.

"It's okay," he interrupted. "You're probably just tired. Sleeping in a truck bed wouldn't have helped that. You can take a nap if you want."

"Sure, yeah. I guess I'll just head up." A nap sounded lovely.

"And I will ring Althea," he assured her.

She watched him glide away as she rubbed her wrist. She stared at the thin jewelry. No signs of glowing red and her wrist and arm now felt fine. Maybe she was just imagining things. It was high past time for a proper shower and a good sleep.

A gentle warmth accompanied the tinge of hope in her stomach as she stepped out of the bathroom. Sure, the clothes were still dirty and torn from her adventure, but after a hot scrub, Ro felt human again. A soft mattress caught her as she flopped down to meet it. Surrounded by fluffy bedding the world seemed anew. Sunlight streamed through the nearby window, casting flecks of dust to dance along her vision. Everything seemed light and, for the first time since this whole mess started, it seemed right. She drifted into a dreamless sleep.

CHAPTER FOUR

An hour later, she was still cozy, hidden away in the overflowing nest of blankets. The incessant doorbell pulled Ro from from sleep as greetings and jovial voices floated upstairs. Peri's friends must have arrived, the ones who could help against the Nefarie. Ro knew she should feel overwhelmed with happiness, excited to get some answers, yet a nagging feeling in her brain would not go away.

With a huff, she sat up, glaring at the blinding sunlight as her stomach twisted with anxiety. How long had it been since she'd fallen from Althea's house? How long since she left Adyra and Ace in that crappy motel on the coast?

A door slammed below, and Ro stood, alert and pulled from her thoughts. Peri was probably waiting for the right moment to come get her, but a little sneak peek wouldn't hurt, right?

She slipped on her shoes and walked out the door, not wanting to sound off any of the old boards on the shiny wooden floor. The voices drifted louder as she tiptoed toward the grand staircase, hunching down behind a low rising wall as not to be seen.

The excited jumble of voices told her they were gathering in the dining hall by the bottom of the marbled stairs. Bits of conversation reached her ears as she willed herself to become as still as possible. "A miracle," one high voice crept over many mms and murmured agreements.

Low chatter cluttered together, and Peri spoke over the crowd. "Believe me, I was just as shocked as you, but proud none-the-less. Soon she'll understand our plight." His cool smugness put Ro's senses on alert.

Were they talking about her? She leaned away in confusion. What plight? Peri said these friends would help, but he sounded cold and almost detached, nothing like the fun-loving godfather of her childhood days. She shook her head, maybe she was just looking for things that weren't there.

"They will be very proud, Pericuios," a deep voice said. "Very happy with you and the young Sparrow"

NO! Ro thought, jumping back. *He wouldn't! It's not possible!* That voice. It would forever be burned into her memory. The same voice that carried through the dark, chasing her into hiding in Althea's room, sending shivers down her spine as she hung back in fear. Her eyes widened with the shock pumping through her frozen body. That person was here, they all were. She had settled into the very snake pit she wanted to avoid.

Adrenaline pulsed though her veins, her brain screaming, *I told you so!* Jumping up from her crouched position, Ro's foot hit the wall that had hidden her. The murmuring voices stopped as she ran down the hallway at full speed.

"Ro?" Peri's voice jumped to surprise. "Sparrow, wait!"

She could hear him rushing toward the stairs. Taking an abrupt right as the hallway ended, Ro found herself in a tall library of books. Light streamed in from the windows as she rushed past a collection of shipping boxes and quickly climbed a ladder to the second story loft. She could hear the commotion, people yelling and barking out orders as doors to various rooms were flung open.

She ran quickly, choosing some stacks to hide behind. *Perfect plan. Head to the very place the ones who attacked me are going to be.* She crouched underneath a wide window, urging her breath to slow as the entrance to the library below swung wide. She knew she was trapped, stuck again, hiding from the very monsters she'd been trying to escape since this thing started. This time though, there were no twisted inky shadows, just beaming sunlight and the dusty smell of old, unturned pages. How did she keep putting herself in these situations?

"Ro," Peri called into the room. "Sweetie, let me explain."

His shoes echoed sharply, mimicking her pounding heart. "Just come out we can talk about this."

She could have laughed from the pure stupidity of this situation had fear not kept her lips glued together.

More people entered the room, searching up and down the rows of books. Did he think she would just come out, blindly trusting him? *Well, you blindly trusted him,* Ro's inner voice criticized. But in her defence, Peri was supposed to be like family. And you didn't betray your family.

She could hear his voice, closer now, perhaps at the end of the stairs. "Ro. It's Peri, you know me."

My parents, she thought, chagrined. *He said he knew what happened to them, that he could provide answers.* He'd greeted her with open arms. Was it all a trap?

Tousled strands of damp hair tickled her cheeks as calculated footsteps entered the second floor.

"Maybe, like her namesake, she did not run. Maybe she flew." The low voice chuckled.

"Shut up, she's here. There's not an exit on this floor," Peri hissed. "Ro," he continued with a kinder tone. "I know you're up here. I just want to talk, to explain. That's why you came to me, right? I've already given you answers to some of your questions, let me help now." He sounded closer as he navigated the stacks.

On her left, a tall figure approached. There was no way she could stay where she had crouched, yet there was nowhere else to run. The sound of people searching the house continued below, but her focus was fixed on that solitary shadow as it drew near. Letting her fear turn into anger, Ro stood, fuelled by months of pain and worry, and by the bitter sting of Peri's betrayal. She unleashed all she had been holding in.

"Explain!?" She stepped out to face her godfather. "You want to explain?" Her eyebrows shot up and her hands tightened into fists.

Peri raised his hands in a gesture of mock surrender, casting what she assumed he thought was a reassuring smile,

"If you would just—"

"No!" She cut him off, shaking from the emotion coursing through her. She was tired of running and annoyed at herself for being so defenceless. "You want to explain what?"

His smile dropped.

"You want to explain what happened to my parents?" she spit at him. "Who trusted you by the way! What about explaining what happened at Althea's, you know, your ex-wife's place?"

He grimaced at her rising voice.

"Or maaaaybeee," she dragged the word out, "you want to explain how you are all of a sudden best friends with the people who attacked me? Explain that, Peri!" Her voice rumbled and her throat burned with the fire of her anger.

The search of the house had ceased and people filed into the library's main level, their presence bolstering Peri's confidence as he approached her. He sighed, feigning empathy. "Ro, sweetheart your parents had the chance to understand. They had the chance to teach you, but they didn't."

Though her anger made her want to lash out, Ro wanted to put as much distance between them as she could. She stepped closer to the wall behind her.

"We won't hurt you. I won't hurt you. You know that." His calm voice mocked her.

How is this the same person who taught me to play soft-ball? Ro wondered.

To Peri's right, the same icy voice from before crawled out from under a pointed hood, like that of her dreams.

"Listen to him, Sparrow, we wish you no harm."

"Yeah, because I'm going to listen to the guy whose biggest achievement is rolling a D20." Probably not the biggest insult for a guy who sounded like he was 80, but it was the best she could come up with. Ro felt her patience wearing thin.

Peri snorted back a chuckle. "Ignore him. You have to trust *me*, Sparrow. Besides, dear, there is really no place to go. Don't you want to be reunited with your family?"

At this point she stood only a few feet from the window. A quick glance back confirmed she was trapped. "You'll forgive me if I don't exactly believe you," she said. "You told me they had a chance to teach me. What does that mean?"

"I spoke with your father for years, giving him, no, giving them both, the chance to understand, but in their own stupidity and self-righteousness they refused to see things as they truly are. Humans are getting the cream of the crop while we waste away, and you can help with that. They just had to share with you, teach you! I want you to know the truth, to understand." He dropped his hands and resumed his idiotic smiling, standing tall as the crowd below filled the room.

That glaring smirk broke something in her, opening a dark pit that swallowed all her fear. This had gone on long enough. Moving slightly, her hand searched for a distraction behind her. Peri continued smiling as he held out his own, gesturing for her to take it. Ro knew if she did, she would have to face everything Ace and Adyra had told her to run from. If she had to choose between them and taking that offering, she would refuse the latter. Everything in her was screaming, urging her to get away. She frantically felt for something, anything. Then she had it, her hand twisted around a heavy object, the perfect tool for helping her cause. Slowly moving away from him, she investigated her godfather's face, one that held the smugness of premature success.

"That's the stupidest thing you've said today," Ro said, gripping the metal-cased book her hand had found. "I don't have any interest in your truth."

With everything she had, Ro hurled it at him, taking some satisfaction in ripping that smile from his face.

Ro watched as his hand shot out in a rage.

"*Volant!*" he cried.

The book took a hard left before smashing to the floor with such force that it split. Pages flew around the metallic shards.

How did… how did he do that?

Ro froze, the book didn't even strike him before he smacked it away. There was no way he could have batted it, especially not with such force. She picked up the book, looking at the remains in shock. It was like he had controlled it with a flick of the wrist and a word. Confusion filled her as she glanced up to the stormy eyes glaring back at her. That had been her one chance to distract him, her slim opportunity to escape. In seconds he had not only destroyed her feeble plan but had done so in such a way that defied all laws of science. It wasn't possible, yet it had happened right in front of her. There had to be an explanation, she reassured herself, this sort of thing didn't happen outside of movies or TV.

Peri's face froze with a look of irritation. He lifted his eyes, his face stormier than she had ever seen it. "That wasn't very polite," he growled as her hope depleted into despair.

There was nothing to do now, nowhere to go but to accept her fate.

"I thought we could handle this as adults." He stepped up to her. "But now I see —"

Tap tap. Something sharp and metal was tapping on the stained glass window.

Ro flinched away from the noise behind her. Peri's focused adverted to the window she had crouched beneath.

Tap tap.

"Oh, you insufferable," he started with a roll of his eyes.

A cracking noise cut him off. Looking up, she saw a long line splitting the stained glass in two, a gleaming arrow pulling it as it embedded itself into the wood of another bookcase.

"What the—?" Ro ducked as the glass came crashing down. Pieces ricocheted off nearby surfaces, somehow not hitting where she stood. Gasping, Ro determined that this was a better distraction than any other. As she prepared to run, a blur whirled into the room, a figure swinging through the broken shards and into the sudden chaos.

Two thick boots made contact with her godfather's chest and with a solid thunk, Peri's body lay in a crumpled heap.

Ro felt a small hand grip her arm as familiar brown eyes focused on her. "We need to go."

"Go…?" she replied, sputtering. "That's kinda what I was trying to do." She felt herself being pulled passed the stacks of books. Her feet worked faster than her mind, pausing for a second as they passed the unconscious Peri before she was tugged forward to the railing.

"He's fine, by the way."

"Who?"

"Peri. He might have a slight concussion when he wakes up, but we both know he deserves much worse." Adyra stood in front of her, frustration etched into her brow as she let Ro go.

"How did you know I was here?" Ro cried.

Instead of responding, the smaller girl just rolled her eyes, shaking her bangs away as she surveyed the room. The house had become a war zone

Figures fought either donned in cloaks or dressed in bright woven cloth, latching onto each other as punches flew and bodies rolled. The library stood in disarray as arrows whooshed and swords clanged. Voices rose together to form a nonsensical chant.

Adyra's eyebrows rose as someone was tossed through the thin wooden ladder, causing it to collapse. "Well, that's no longer an option."

Ro could taste smoke and watched as a shelf and its contents went up in flames

"What do we do?" She turned to face her friend.

Adyra wore the same outfit of bright cloth as others fighting below. With a sigh, she turned to Ro. "Jump."

"What?" Ro protested. Adyra had always been just shy of a few marbles.

"Either you jump, or I'll push you. The floor isn't that far, although if you want the take the second option, I'd be more than happy to oblige." She radiated iciness. "We don't have time for you to contemplate," Adyra shouted.

Arrows flew by and Ro dodged out the way of a thrown body.

Her stomach lurched as she ungracefully lunged over the banister. Desperately, she tried to grab the air that flew through her fingertips. Bracing herself for impact, Ro closed her eyes against the floor rushing toward her.

Slowly, she opened her eyes. It wasn't the cold hard floor that had broken her fall. Collapsed around her, she recognized the faint manila colouring of shipping boxes that had been laying empty before she tumbled into them. With the sudden rush of her senses catching up to her, Ro choked on the oxygen she fought to regain and she groaned. Screams echoed, increasing as the ground shook from a crash to the left. Her back cried out as she twisted to regain her sense of balance, and two hands shot into her cave to pull her up.

The air was dirtier on the main floor of the library and she fought to make out her friend through the smoke.

"That was not a good idea," she muttered. It felt like she had bruised her whole arm.

"Oh, you're fine, don't be so melodramatic."

"Dramatic?" she cried, feet stumbling over the shaking ground. "And you're perfectly fine after a fall like that?" Ro came to a halt, the smoke in the air starting to block her vision.

"The boxes were there, and it's no worse than when we used to jump down from the treehouse as kids." Adyra yelled hoarsely over the chaos around them.

"I broke my arm doing that!" Ro reminded her.

Adyra's only response was a snort, and to Ro's astonishment, she pulled an arrow from her quiver, firing it off in the direction of their path. The ground shook again, and Ro could hear someone curse in front of them.

"Is that a bow?" she asked as they continued forward. "I thought you were passive; you know, non-violence?"

Adyra smirked as they left the library, racing through cloaked figures and clamouring swords. "Yeah well, fighting to survive is better than dying, I've been told. Besides, you'd be surprised at how many conflicts this bow can stop." She suddenly halted, causing Ro to slam against her back.

Dense smoke weighed them down, pushing the breath out of Ro's lungs and resting heavy on her chest. The ground constantly shook, the cursing and screams from the battle scene getting louder. Adyra stood, blocking Ro with her stance as she calmly drew her bow, aiming dead ahead. Through the mayhem, a figure drifted into sight, rounding up the last of the staircase. Though bodies flew passed, the person remained untouched as he gracefully moved closer.

"Sparrow…" The same voice from Claudaith crawled toward her again. "Only you can stop this chaos." A thick hand slid out as he gestured to the violence encircling the room.

"Let us pass, old man, before things get ugly." Adyra drew herself up, moving to cover Ro even more.

"Oh, you silly fool," he sighed. "You're nothing but a poor disgraced child whose parents couldn't bear the sight of you."

"Either you move, or I'll make you move," she called forcefully.

"Listen to her," Ro pushed out, refusing to let her friend face this alone. "Let us pass."

His eerie chuckle sounded over them. "Try it, orphan" His words floated on dying air. "Let us see who's left standing." He halted a few feet away as ash drifted in the air. "Besides, when you're gone, who do you think will be guarding her?"

"He's right," Adyra whispered. She took a step, forcing them back and closer to the edge of the landing.

"I can defend myself!" Ro insisted as she looked at the confusion and despair all around her.

"You saw what Peri did to that book right?" Adyra pushed.

Ro's blood turned to ice again at the memory.

"Well, this guy is a lot older; he can do more than some simple parlour trick."

The ground shook and Ro grasped onto the half wall separating her from the floor below. "If you're fighting him then I am not leaving you alone to do so. This guy's problem is apparently with me, not you."

Adyra sighed at this. "I hate to be stereotypical and ask if you trust me, Ro, but screw it, you gotta have some faith in me. We need to get you as far away from here as possible."

"Again. Not happening."

The whole house bellowed, swaying as the standoff continued.

"Jump." Adyra motioned to the level below.

"I'm sorry, what?" Ro's voice broke.

"Jump."

"This is further than before. I'm not leaving you!" She stumbled, trying to keep what little balance she held.

"Then you're just going to have to forgive me, although it is kind of cathartic after the stunt you pulled in Aylee." Adyra smirked as she spun around quickly.

Before Ro could react, Adyra seized her waist,

launching her over the half wall that separated the first and second floor.

Ro felt her body giving away to gravity again as she flew.

Before her vision was distorted by a cloud of ash, Ro watched the smaller girl fire an arrow then call out, "Ace, you're up!"

CHAPTER FIVE

hy was she always falling? Plummeting in her nightmares, tumbling into hidden tunnels, diving from landings? Ro found herself rapidly speeding downward, unwillingly chased by darkness. The same inky black that had consumed the house. At this point she was over the fear, fuming at these abrasive forces that were taking over her average life. Anger pulsed through Ro as her arms caught in the wind, unable to stop or control the vicious cycle. Adyra had taken the choice away when she refused to jump after her, and now it seemed the heavy dark was absorbing the very spot they had stood above.

She suddenly jerked forward, greeted not by the cool tiled floor but something — someone — catching her sideways in a steely grip. A crash sounded nearby as the earth startled, convulsing beneath them. Thick wisps of dirty blond hair hung over the left side of Ace's stormy face. He tilted her up and Ro once again aligned her feet with the vibrating floor. "Nice of you to drop in," he said.

"Thanks for the flyby landing," she huffed with annoyance, secretly grateful it had been him to catch her, and not one of the others. The ground tilted again as another hooded figure leapt toward them.

"We need to go!" Ace grunted, drawing a sword and quickly launching the attacker away. With a thud, the cloaked figure flew off to the side and landed in the dense smoke across the room.

"Not without Adyra!" Ro coughed through the carbon monoxide.

The clanging continued around them as they dodged and ducked around various bodies.

"She's fine," he called. "She can handle her own, trust me."

Everything rattled as he latched onto her arm. "You see the smoke?" he shouted. "This whole place is going to crumble."

Ro went to pull away, unwilling to leave their friend behind when the earth groaned, shaking with such force the staircase crashed into itself, breaking apart in jagged marble bits.

Engaged fighters tumbled into the abyss.

A whistle jerked their eyes upwards.

"Told you," he muttered in her ear.

Above them, Adyra flipped through the haze, landing crouched in dirt-ridden leggings. "Why are you still here?" she exclaimed. "Why is she still here?"

Her glare bore into them as Ace shifted. "We don't have time!" The ground shook in anger as a large crack shot through the floor between them.

"Let's go!"

Metallic smoke bellowed into Ro's lungs as she turned to run, fighting to follow them through the murky haze. Her ears throbbed with the shuddering of the house as she pushed her tired legs to keep up.

Adyra's retreating form pushed her to sprint faster through the screams.

Arrows flew as Ace ran alongside her, his sword glinting with readiness, prepared to attack anyone who came too close. It felt like they were becoming entrapped, the room becoming less and less visible as heavy fumes churned and swirled, producing the thick dark substance that nipped at their heels. Suddenly, Ace was urging her through the wrecked entry and into the barren driveway.

"A car!" he yelled. "We can't escape them on foot."

The wind picked up, whipping hair into her eyes as she struggled to stay with them. Ro's chest screamed for air as she sprinted through the dirt and rocks, her feet slipping with every step.

"On your right," she heard Adyra call as the petite girl whipped around, firing an arrow just past them.

"Focus to the front, cover our backs, then regroup," Ace yelled beside her.

"What?" Ro's confused brain sluggishly processed their words.

"Not you!" came their combined shouts.

Adyra waited for them to catch up, holding a vehicle door open. "Get in!" she demanded.

Ace nodded, racing around the black SUV, silver trimmings glinting with the orange reflection of a fire. Ro slid into the passenger seat, quickly buckling up.

"Nice upgrade." She gestured to the high-end technology on the dashboard.

Ace's only response was a chuckle as the vehicle rumbled to life.

"I'll have the Praesidium continue the distraction and meet you just past the border," Adyra told him, gripping the handle to hold her balance. "We will make contact at Eclipsglade when we can."

Ro watched as Ace passed a quiver from behind his seat to Adyra.

"You're staying to fight them?" Ro exclaimed, bewildered.

Adyra smirked. "Can't let the boys have all the fun out there."

"Stay safe." Ace flashed her a grin. "That's an order."

With a laugh, Adyra slammed the door. Ro flew forward, gripping the dash as Ace slammed on the gas and they whipped out of the driveway.

She leaned back, both hands now dead-locked onto the leather seat. "I'm going to go out on a limb and make a guess here that this isn't the first time either of you have done this?" she said.

The SUV bumped along an old road, trees and scenery blending at their unsafe speed.

He laughed. "Not exactly."

She grimaced. "Well, now that we're in this lovely situation, care to explain?"

"Explain what?"

"Don't play coy with me, Aceius." Her tone held an unusual growl.

His hands grew white with pressure as he swerved to avoid debris and her questions.

"What about the Praesidium?" she asked.

The vehicle veered, moving to avoid a massive pot-hole.

"The archers?"

"Archers?"

"Yes," he grunted. "The Praesidium are archers."

"Like Adyra?"

The sky shifted, starting to grey.

"The archers are a separate division that protect our kind. Including Adyra." His eyes squinted toward her for a fleeting second before he shifted gears, pressing the car to go even faster.

"Our kind?" Her brain stuttered as he sighed.

"Give me moment, Ro. I'm trying to focus; you know life or death here and all."

As serious as the situation was, she couldn't help the snort that flew out of her as the SUV screeched with fury.

Ace slammed the wheel violently to the left as they fishtailed onto a small, paved path.

"Aaaaace…" She drew his name out, attempting to find the right words.

"What?" he muttered as they reached a steady speed.

"Nothing"

"Nothing never means nothing with you."

"Well, now it does!" she snapped.

"Not this again." He groaned.

"Not what?"

"Let me guess? You're mad? Again? And now you're stuck with me. Again." His voice drifted through the vehicle as the earth rumbled around them.

He tried to catch her eyes, but they were determinedly avoiding him.

Ro bit her lip, ruminating on the past two days. She wasn't refusing to answer, just finding herself unable to. Trees mushed together into boring greenery as the sky continued to darken. Out the side mirror she saw the war they left behind as a dark cloud. She gripped the leather seat and squeezed her eyes tight to pretend she was anywhere but there.

A troubling thought pierced the anxiety... this was her life now.

Running from unseen forces, being chased in fear. Everything she had known had been ripped away, leaving her with nothing but uncertainty. Her friends suddenly wielding weapons, an enraged group hunting her, and people she thought she could trust being the source of betrayal. *Seriously, what did Peri do to that stupid book?* Ro bounced in her seat as they swerved to the left, Ace's defeated groan caused her eyes to open.

"Look," he said. "I can't promise to explain everything just yet, but if you're willing to listen, willing to open that door of yours to forgiving me, then I can explain some things from my side, okay?"

It wasn't everything she wanted, but his tired tone taunted her curiosity, and she gave in. "Okay, tell me your side then." She turned to face him. "Maybe you can include why you weren't there for me the one time I needed you guys the most? I texted you and texted you. We were supposed to meet up that day, remember? Then, just like my memories, you were gone. All I got was radio silence and that horrible text... Even Adyra wasn't that harsh." She folded her arms over her chest and her eyes flashed in pain. If they were going to do this, she was certain they were going to do it right and put everything out on the table.

"You're hurt, Ro. I get it, I do, and I really am sorry if that counts for anything."

"I'm listening, aren't I?" She shifted a bit as they jerked suddenly to the left, avoiding a limb that had fallen in the chaos around them.

"I had to cut contact with you. I don't know what you have pieced together, but there was a group assigned to protect you after your parents' attack. Our lines were being monitored, personal phones and all. We knew there was a mole and we didn't have a clue who it was. I wasn't going to risk anyone finding you on Claudaith and was assigned to strengthening the barrier around you."

"A group?" she murmured.

"Your parents and mine were —" He shifted his tone

with a look at her. "—are really good friends. They have been since before you and I ever came into the picture. There have always been people protecting you, Ro. You just didn't know it."

"Why would I need protection?"

His tone was heavy. "When your parents moved to Enderson Beach they cut all connections they had, with the exception of Peri, Althea, and us."

"Those other connections… were they the same ones that sent me to Claudaith Island with Althea?"

His face scrunched up to meet her gaze as if he was chewing on a lemon peel.

"I can't tell you yes just yet, but I am not going to lie and say no. I can reiterate though, that from day one I've always had your back. So has Adyra; in fact, she was put in your life for your own protection, she just happened to become friends with us in the process— and believe me, that's not an easy thing for her."

"*Placed* into my life? What does that even mean?" Ro asked, shocked.

"I can explain better when we get there."

"Get where?"

"Soon," he promised, twisting the wheel to avoid another tree in the road. "Those… people, for lack of a better word, I guess—the ones who are after you—they think you can help them with something, something very bad. Evil even. Something that would have horrible consequences. That's why your family left with you, that's why we're protecting you now."

"How could I possibly help them?"

"The point is, they think you can."

With another haphazard turn, they started to bounce even more. Ro steadied herself with the door handle, listening.

"You have to understand, when your parents were attacked, we were underprepared. Althea took you into hiding and we worked to strengthen the barrier between you and them."

"You?" She was stunned, her thoughts swimming in this new information. "What happened that day?"

"I'm going to get in so much trouble for this," he said, sighing. "This group, they have been after you since the moment you were born. They were trying to bring you in, but your mom and dad fought hard. You'll see them again, Ro." He looked her way, a fierceness shining in his softening eyes. "I promise."

She glanced at the mirror again, the smoke they'd left behind lost in the darkness. "You said you worked to strengthen the barrier? What does that mean?"

Silence was held for a moment in the front seat as they both took deep breaths.

"Adyra was allowed communication with you, updating me on the situation, but I couldn't contact you because we were working day and night to make sure that the barrier around Claudaith stayed up."

"So those nights she mentioned you had no sleep?"

"None of us had. "

"And this barrier?"

"Ro..." He sounded exasperated. "Think about it. All of a sudden, weird things start happening. Your parents disappeared and your memories were stolen. You go to live with Althea on some island you've never even heard of that was so close to where you once lived. Daylight turns to nighttime as this thick black inky substance surrounds everything and hounds after you. You are chased into hiding, and all of a sudden, your godfather betrays you. What changed in your life before that?"

"My birthday," she muttered.

"Oooooor…" He dragged the word out with a wide-eyed look. "Have weird things always happened and you were just taught to ignore it? You're smart enough to put two and two together. Come on, think about it, Ro!" His voice frayed as they violently bounced down the path.

The ride was feeling wilder by the moment as she gripped permanent fingermarks into the seat, the belt biting into her. *Think about it,* he had said, and she was thinking about it. The events of the past few days clashed in her brain as she looked out at the unnaturally dark sky. A chill drifted toward her even though the AC wasn't on, and she turned to glance at the mirror again in shock.

The darkness they had left was now right behind them. Thick ominous clouds rushed toward the car, surrounding the sky, and eating the sun.

"Ace," she called.

"No, Ro, listen!" he rambled. "I know you're mad, but—"

"Ace!" she tried to interject again.

"Just think about it, all these happenings and —"

"Aceius!" she shouted. "Behind us!"

He finally paused, seeing her fear and jerking the wheel again in exasperation. "What is the Praesidium doing?" He let out a frustrated growl. "Ro, I need you to listen to me very carefully." His tone simmered, low and deadly.

"I'm listening," she grunted back, bracing herself on the dash once more.

"Do you see that tree there?" Up ahead, the road curved, passing a clearing of green grass leading to a forest still touched by sunlight. "Take off your seat belt and —"

"Um, how about no," she argued.

"I wouldn't tell you to do anything that wasn't safe," he insisted.

"Not safe?"

"When I stop in that clearing up there, you're going to get out and run to that tree as fast as you can without looking back. When I give the word, unbuckle, and start running."

"What about you?"

"Don't worry about me. I'll be right there, just run, okay?"

"Toward that tree; and once I get there?"

It stood taller than the rest, a vine-like bark twisting up its abnormally broad trunk.

"Just get to the tree, okay? There's a part that looks like it's been struck by lightning, almost like there's a caved area inside the base, head there."

"But what about the — ?"

"No but's," Ace barked, cutting her off. "Please trust me, okay? Head there and try to empty your brain off all thoughts. Try not to think of anything. Picture a white, empty box, okay?"

She nodded as they jostled onto the grass.

"Now!" he cried, slamming the car into park, and twisting the wheel all the way to the left.

Ro undid her belt and gripped the door.

"And Ro," —he met her eyes with an earnest intensity— "You're more important than you think."

She bounded out the door, fighting not to look at the sky breaking behind her.

The tree became clearer as she raced against the dimming sun. Ace was right, as she was almost there, it appeared the centre of the trunk had been burnt out, charred edges creating an entryway. The ground rumbled as the sky bellowed and she rushed toward the dark opening. What she would do when she got there, Ro didn't know.

With burning lungs, she focused on her efforts. The smell of smoke accompanied the winds and she pushed herself even further. When it felt like her legs were begging to give out, she reached the trunk. Before she could enter, hands wrapped around her, pushing them both into the entrance with a heavily whispered, *"Eclipsi."*

She focused on that word, concentrating hard not to think of any certain place like he had said. Then, with a frosty whoosh, they were gone.

CHAPTER SIX

Everything hurt. Instead of hitting the inside of the trunk with her face, Ro found herself slamming into a patch of rocky, damp earth. Standing on unsteady legs, she pressed her palms into her eyes. Adjusting to her surroundings, she swallowed thickly, her stomach churning angrily. With a groan, she stretched her thin arms. Wind had whipped back her hair, making it slash at her dirt-ridden face and neck before settling messily into place. An icy chill burned her skin when she entered the tree and, for a moment, she could have sworn they were in the dead of winter, but as she looked around, Ro realized the air was warm. Ace was on his knees a few feet away, digging through a small bag.

It was difficult to explain what she was seeing, as her brain struggled to catch up. They were standing in a forest thick with shimmering evergreen trees. There was no crazy storm, no one chasing them, no sign of the road they had just been on. Confused, she turned, seeing a nearly identical tree to the one she had entered moments earlier. Its towering trunk seemingly covered in an early morning dew. Ro tiptoed around the tree, looking for any sign of where they came from.

"I know." Ace bellowed out a laugh as he stood. "Amazing, isn't it? I had the same reaction the first time I used the Vindden."

No one could blame her for the rambling reaction that followed. "We're—?" She took a moment to look around again. "Where are we? What happened? Vindden? I don't… what?" Her wide, bright eyes met his amused expression.

"Okay, shake it off, girl." He grinned. "A Vindden is the transportation tree, linking both realms. It's this huge, marvellous thing here." He clapped his hand against it. "It's a means of travel. Remember when I said not to think of any place if possible?"

She nodded numbly, working hard to process this information.

"Well, that was so we would wind up where *I* was thinking. You see, the Vindden grants those with the blood seal permission to travel to the destinations they approve. Sure, there have been some accidents in the past with more than one person travelling at once, but as long as you weren't thinking of any place different than I was, and we both had good intentions, then I knew we would end up right where we needed to be."

"And this is…" she started, grasping at his words.

"This is how we got here? That huge tree you had me run toward transported us to this forest?"

"Yep, welcome to Eclipsi."

"It lets those with a blood seal have passage through to another place… like a strange, blood-related teleportation device?" An alarming thought rang through the confusion. "What if they followed us?" she cried, arms shooting out as she scanned the area around them.

"They couldn't have," Ace promised. "There was no way that they could have known that I was thinking of here."

"Adyra said it, remember? At Peri's before we left in the SUV, you said she would meet us here!"

"Nope. She said Eclipsglade. That's the clearing where we came through." He smiled reassuringly. "But there was so much chaos that no one could have overheard us anyway. They were much more concerned with getting to you, and she was the only one who knew of the plan to take you here as the safe point. This location was randomly picked, so on the off chance that something happened, even if they try, they can't break the information out of her."

The words resounded in her mind. *Even if they tried to break her.* They being the Nefarie, Adyra being the one they might break. Panic shot through her and she gaped at Ace's calmness. "If she was supposed to be here by the time we left, then where is she? Do they have her?" Ro's mind raced as her blood pressure rose. She could not let her friend be caught for protecting her!

Seeing her fear, Ace placed both hands on her shoulders. "She okay, Ro."

His words waded through her sea of worries. "How do you know?"

"How do you think I got this stash bag? She left it for us."

"Stash bag?" Ro looked at the lumpy sack he swung around. He produced a few flowing fabrics, tossing a loose pile toward her face. "No hand-eye coordination, remember?" She glared as he laughed at her stumbling catch as half the items landed at her feet.

"Change," he said. "And when you're ready, we'll be on our way."

The cloth felt soft, an unusual mixture of light and heavy textures in her hands.

She gestured to the dirtied jeans and t-shirt she had been travelling in. "Isn't what I'm wearing okay?" she asked.

Giving her the once over, he smirked. "Sure, stay in that if you want to stick out. But these clothes will help you blend in. The best way through a situation is not being a sore thumb."

"And you?" she asked, sparing a glance at his somehow still clean fighting garb.

"I," he emphasized, raising a hand to show his clothes, "am changing too. Right over there." He gestured to a heavily wooded area to his right. "So, if you want to change and meet me here when you're done, we can head out."

On the one hand, Ro thought she wouldn't mind a

clean set of clothing; her mud-stained shirt had dried to her skin long ago. On the other hand, she was stubborn and wanted to cling to that normalcy.

"Okay, fine," she relented. "I'll change and meet you here, on one condition."

"Of course," he muttered, arching a brow.

"Over the past two days I have seen shadows move, objects tossed aside with some whispered words, and a tree that somehow teleported us out of there. You said that some mysterious group was after me and I've spent my whole life being hidden and protected without knowing it. This game of half answers is getting old. It's my life. I should have a say. You give me some answers and then we leave."

Ro crossed her arms confidentially as he rolled his eyes with a sigh.

"Fine, I'll see what I can do about providing you with answers. Go. Change. We will talk on the way."

Spinning away from him, she marched into the brush past the Vindden with a huff. Ro knew the sooner she met back up with Ace the closer she was to figuring out what in the world was going on, so she might as well do as he asked. She refused to remain in the dark.

Feeling discreet enough behind the foliage, Ro turned her attention to the soft fabrics in her hand. Separating the pieces onto a nearby branch, she laid them out to make sense of their odd shapes and quickly started to redress. Dark red pooled seamlessly to her knees as she slid on the first piece. The neckline was high on the dress. She blew out an annoyed breath, tossing her jeans aside. Turtlenecks always felt like they were choking her. Ro smoothed down the waist.

She was startled to find a small dagger tucked into the mesh design. How had she not seen that when putting it on? With such thin fabric she should have felt cold, but the dress seemed to radiate heat as it clung to her. Taking a deep breath, Ro picked up the next two objects. To her surprise, what appeared to be stockings tumbled into two blue, silver trimmed boots. If this was the way people dressed here, then her stale clothing wouldn't have blended in at all. On the upside, Ro was pretty sure she had never owned anything that felt so nice before.

If the people they had escaped knew what she looked like, then how would this attempt at blending in help? Sure, the dress appeared more like a jumpsuit and that made her happy, and the shoes might have been the most comfortable pair she had ever worn, but all that meant nothing if the point was to disguise her. Rolling her eyes, she reached for the smallest piece of fabric, expecting a scarf or something. To her amazement, that tiny square came apart, heavily draping around her into an inky pool. Unlike the other clothes, it hung heavier and thicker, an inky blue dripping to the grass below. So blue, in fact, under the right light, Ro could have sworn it was black. She had seen this before, wrapped around her pursuers, although this one was much lighter and had a normal hood, one that didn't slice down to a point. Suddenly, Ro was filled with under-standing: she wasn't meant to match, but to hide her looks altogether. After all, no one could recognize you, or even know who you were, if they couldn't see your defining features.

Slipping on the heavy cloak and sliding the hood to her shoulders, Ro was surprised again at how comfortable it was. She expected to be dragged down by the weight of it, but instead stood tall under the soft, slow-moving fabric.

Grumbling about the difficulty of walking back through the woods, Ro grabbed her old clothes and headed back to the Vindden. She knew that getting snagged on a branch and falling into a broken limb would be just her luck on a day like this, so she lifted the cloak as to not trip.

No less resolute, she marched forward to the meeting place, to Ace, and to the answers she was determined to get. Some might say she marched forward, headstrong, ready to accept her destiny, but she didn't know what that meant just yet.

CHAPTER SEVEN

Pushing thick branches aside, Ro emerged from the thicket to find Ace sitting casually on the path.

"Have fun?" he called.

"Oh, a blast." She was too tired for this, and she gave him her old clothes quickly. "Why is this necessary again?"

"This is how people dress here. One look at street clothes and someone would call you out for sure." He put their dirty clothing into the old sack.

"So, people here just walk around in cloaks like that's no big creepy ordeal?"

"It's not creepy." He laughed. "They radiate warmth, adjusting appropriately to your body temp and the outside air. Besides, I'm in a cloak too, see?" With this, Ace gestured to the light green fabric that spilled out around him.

As much as she hated to admit it, Ace was right. She did feel better seeing he had changed as well, although she couldn't really see his other clothes past the cloak. A flash of green and blue here and there along with some dark shiny shoes.

He fastened the sack to his waist. "Alright. Let's go."

Ro caught his arm, stopping him from continuing their little adventure. "Not so fast, Aceius." A proud smile piggybacked onto her words. "You promised to give me some answers. Your cloak explanation only added to my growing list."

His shoulders shifted downwards as he turned with determination. "I did, and I will." He sighed. "But we should get a move on. It's not smart to linger in one place. How about I answer whatever questions you ask as we're travelling?"

With skeptical eyes she turned toward the Vindden again. "Okay, as long as were not..."

His bellowing laughter cut her off. "Nope, we're walking like normal people today, I'm afraid."

They shared a smile and Ro followed him down the sunlit path.

So much had happened and she wanted to start with a good question. She wanted to pick a smart one, something to ease into him telling her what was really going on.

"Okay, first, where is this mysterious place we're going?"

"Eveningston Estate."

Rocks slid around them as they began their trek down the grassy path. The name clicked something inside of her as Ro cocked her head at the memories dredging up from her past. "Eveningston? As in *you*?" she asked.

"I grew up there, so I would certainly hope so," he replied sarcastically.

"Why call it an estate?"

"Don't really know. It's a family house and that's just what we call it." Ace turned to look at her, serious for a moment. "I know I haven't really checked, but you're okay with going there, right? I promised I wouldn't put you in danger, but if you're uncomfortable, we can figure something else out."

Her thoughts turned slowly. "Your family can help us against the Nefarie?"

"That's why the plan is to take you there," Ace answered. "Besides, my mom would love to see you, she was really upset when the news of your parents reached us, and I've received notice of her fretting about you ever since. You know how she gets when she worries."

The memory of a smaller middle-aged women came to Ro's mind—one who loved to bake and was always finding something to clean. The kind of person who seemed too small to make much notice of herself, but the moment you upset her was the instant you knew to regret it, and that almost always happened when she was concerned about those she cared for.

A sense of relief came with the recollection of summer trips, running around the house and sitting by the fire as her mother and Ace's mother gossiped, giggling loudly into the darkening sky—memories she was grateful to have. She was more than comfortable going to see Ace's parents. They had always loved her and treated her like their own.

Her mind was made up. "I would love to see your parents, Ace," she said as they came to a crossing.

"Good," Ace said, leading her to the path that deviated to the left. "We should be there soon. Are you sure you want to waste your questions on my family home?"

He tossed a teasing smile as she picked up the conversation. "No, I was just getting started."

Though they were somewhat joking now, Ro didn't fail to notice Ace never truly let his guard down. As they walked together, he did look relaxed, but he was consistently alert, scanning the forest and surrounding areas. Ro also took note of the fact that his left hand rested close to his sword in case of an attack. Worry raced through her, but she pushed it down again to continue her questions. After all, knowledge might help her the most right now.

"Those people, the ones who are after me, who are they?"

Ace's grin dropped, although he still walked with a relaxed demeanour. "I suppose, since we're far enough into Valerie now... They call themselves the Nefarie, as you know. Originally, they were known as the Nefariu, but the name didn't stick, and it changed over the years."

"And who are they?"

"I wish I could tell you for sure. They are a group who gather with the worst intentions imaginable. When I was a child, they were really nothing more than an old wives' tale, a scary story your parents would speak of to get you to do your chores and be on your best behaviour. Even then, they were still operating, working to commit horrible acts of evil, sneaking and twisting their way through society. Over the past decade, they have grown stronger, using the shadows to hide their dirty work."

The image of her earlier dream drifted to her mind: two cloaked people whispering by a river, covered by the shroud of night, and Ro found herself briefly freezing. *The Nefarie will rise,* the hidden figure had said.

"You okay?" Ace asked, slowing beside her.

"Yeah, fine. Just remembering some weird dream I had."

"About the Nefarie?"

Ro paused, cautious to give out the information, even though she thought she could trust Ace.

"I think so," she finally said. "I don't really know. Anyway, if they are so bad then why doesn't the government shut them down?"

And although Ace peered at her as if he could see behind her façade, he obliged in answering. "They're trying to. The problem is, the Nefarie hasn't ever been publicly announced as a threat. It's a slippery group. People know and speak of them, but no one really confirms their existence." He shrugged. "Other than the politics of it, the problem is that they are good at covering up any possibility of them being recognized, and they're really careful to only show themselves under the secrecy of night. There has only ever been one reported Nefarie sighting in the day, and that was what happened with you."

Even though a warm breeze danced past them, Ro felt nothing but the freeze that seeped into her bones. The very thought that the Nefarie could be anyone, anything, terrified her.

"So, anybody could be part of the Nefarie? It could be your neighbour, or a family member, and you may not even know it?"

"Take Peri for example," Ace said. "You've known him your whole life; so have I. Did you ever expect him to pull that stunt?"

Ro thought back to all the carefree childhood memories she had with the many Christmases and birthdays. Campfires with her whole family. All of it contraindicated with the hardened face her godfather had shown her in the library. Had she not come down early, crashing his gathering, she might have learned too late.

"How did you and Adyra know to be there?" she murmured, fixing her eyes on the flowers beside a nearby pond.

"We didn't, well not for sure. Peri and Althea had a falling out years ago,"

"Yeah, she practically hates him." Ro felt stupid at her easy belief in Peri.

"Well, no one really knows why, but the day they separated, your dad also got into an altercation with him."

This additional information came as a shock. "Dad? I never heard of any fights between them. He always said Peri chose to stay away because it was awkward with Althea. She won us in the divorce or whatever."

"Well…" He cleared his throat. "The way my parents told it, there was such a commotion between the two of them, your dad banned Peri from ever stepping foot in the house again—more specifically, from ever contacting you."

"Me? So, Dad knew? That Peri was in the Nefarie?"

"I'm not sure, he never said if he did, and I'm pretty sure he would've," Ace said. "It was enough though that we had our suspicions and wanted to keep you as far from him as possible. When notice was received about their attack on you and your parents, we knew that your positions had been compromised, and we gathered to relocate you in Claudaith for the time being."

Annoyance pushed through her cloudy confusion. "Why do you do that?" she muttered.

"Do what?"

"You speak as if this is a great game of chess, positions this and replanting that. No one talks like that."

"Sorry." He squinted against the beaming sun. "I've been undercover for months now, hanging around others who speak that lingo. I'm not trying to make this harder for you."

"I know," Ro said softly. "But I'm not some asset. It's my life, not some military game. I need you to speak to me like a normal person. You have to understand that

I am still trying to wrap my head around you even being in a situation that requires you to go undercover. Besides, we've been friends far too long for that."

A teasing grin cracked his stony features as Ace sifted through her words. "So we're friends again?" The sentence was drawn out teasingly as he bumped her shoulder.

Try as she might, Ro couldn't stop her own small smile from peeking out. "Don't push your luck," she said, fighting to impersonate a stern tone. "There are still some things I don't understand though. You said you were undercover? That Althea was planted in my life?"

"Placed, not planted." He sighed. "But I need you to know our friendship with you was never fake. Adyra has had a difficult life, she wouldn't be your friend if she didn't mean it. We're both your friends."

Suddenly, Ace stilled, his left-hand motioning for her to stop as well. In confusion Ro looked at him, catching the light shift in his eyes as he pulled her into a nearby thicket.

"What?" she whispered, bewildered.

"Hood up," he grunted, his dark tone causing her to crouch even lower beside him.

Slipping the hood over her hair, Ro peered through the branches at her eye level.

Down the path in front of them came the cause of his abrupt halt. A younger woman, obviously focused keenly on something in her hands, marched past them. Her steps slowed as she moseyed along, enjoying a leisurely stroll. Her steps shifted the loose dirt on the ground as she moved further away from them, pulling her hair into a tight bun.

"We're near the village," Ace whispered into her ear.

He stood, pulling Ro out of her frozen state with him. That woman… when she pulled her hair up, Ro could have sworn… But it couldn't be… could it?

"Come on," Ace said, interrupting her thoughts. "We need to blend in. Follow me. Keep your head down and hood up.

"Wait…" Ro called as he started down the path again. "Her skin… was it blue?"

Ace's back was turned to her as she raced to catch up.

"It was! She had blue skin! Not like smurf blue, of course, but like light blue, barely there blue. and those markings…"

Her words were cut off as she smashed face first into his still figure.

"We need to look as unassuming as possible," he said. "If we make a scene, we risk alerting anyone who is a part of the Nefarie. You're going to see things that are normal here but not to you, the best thing you can do is act unaffected."

The seriousness of the situation dawned on her again and Ro simply nodded, tabling the questions for later.

"Okay?" he pushed.

"Fine." She covered her features with the hood as Ace flipped his upwards as well.

They moved cautiously, Ro making sure to keep her head low. Although it might have helped if she knew what normal was here, she focused her attention on walking.

No longer able to see Ace's face, she made sure to keep him in her sights as the path they were on widened to reveal a damp alley in between two stone buildings. The noise of everyday life danced to meet her ears.

Passing under a small wooden awning, Ro gulped down her nerves. Knowing this would bring her closer to her family and closer to the truth, she clung to any courage she had and stepped into the bustling city before her. She had come too far to turn back now; she didn't even know that turning back was an option. One thing was sure though, it was now or never, and never was not an option she was willing to accept.

CHAPTER EIGHT

here was an energy in the city unlike anything else. Voices chimed together
in merriment as cars and horses passed. The
stone ground beneath them sprawled into various tents and booths set up in the centre of what appeared to be a market. An assortment of smells made
Ro's nose twitch and mouth water as they stumbled
along. Though clouds hung over the sun in a general
moodiness, laughter could be heard all around as voices
bounced off one another. It was almost impossible to
discern the merging conversations.

"Oh, lovely choice," a vendor said. "That one's on
sale at the moment."

Ro slipped in between the crowds, attempting to
play follow-the-leader with Ace.

A short stubby man gestured to another, scrambling
to fill a bag. "Fresh as always, I promise," he said.

"Though between you and me, it would make it a lot easier to get these crops here if they just got rid of those insolent Bakru."

Biting her lip, she easily mixed with the crowds. If anything, she looked a bit plain. People glided by in massive coats, silk banded pants, and bejewelled dresses. Every now and then, another would pass hidden in their own elaborate cloak, making her and Ace seem normal, and to Ro's amazement, her eyes weren't playing any tricks. All around them, people drifted by with skin the colour of the ocean on a sunny day, or the brightest multi-chromatic eyes that should have been impossible. Tripping as they moved around a lady with sharp pointy ears, Ro allowed Ace to steer her away from the jostling group and down a quieter road.

The urge to talk was overwhelming as she watched with widened eyes, absorbing as much as possible of this new world. She definitely wasn't at home anymore, and any menial hope that this adventure was nothing more than a crazy dream was lost. With that thought, she looked down, worry and guilt dancing across her brow. She had been so caught up in what she was seeing that Ro found herself forgetting for a moment why she was here in the first place. *I will find out what happened that night,* Ro thought, refusing to continue being led around like a sheep in the dark. Whatever else was thrown at her, no matter what, she could handle it.

Tall buildings winding into the sky braced them on both sides, and the stone path turned to stained wood. Some shops blinked with glittering lights as music floated from open windows. A man's singing bounced and blended with another's happy laughter as they rounded a corner. Taking a deep breath, she forced herself to relax. This had to be the right path. Something in her sang at the sight of each twinkling, shop-adorned street. As a young couple passed, Ro found herself so caught up in their outfits adorned with frolicking animals that she failed to notice Ace slowing to match her pace.

"Doven's a pretty amazing place, isn't it?"

She jumped. "Doven?" Something about the name felt right on her tongue.

"Welcome to Doven." He made a grand sweeping gesture. "Small town people, big city attitude."

"Were those…?" A deep breath helped to collect her thoughts. "Were the animals on her dress moving?"

She could almost hear the mischievous grin hidden under his tone. "Maybe. Did they look like they were moving to you?"

Her face scrunched in a grimace at his rhetorical response. "You said we were in Doven?"

"Yeah, it's one of the few towns around here where anyone of any kind can find themselves living peacefully."

"Any kind? Like the lady with pointed ears?"

They took another graceful turn, slowing to a stroll. To anyone else it would appear they were just two peo-ple out for a leisurely walk. "What do you think? " he asked. "Best guesses only."

"Pointed ears make me think of Elves… but that would just be silly, right?"

After a pregnant pause his eyes gleamed over to hers, lips stretched thin as he gave a quick affirming nod. "We're not too far from my place now. I used to spend weekends in Doven as a kid. Or pretty much anytime that I was home from the Halls of Ivy." At least it was an answer.

"The Halls of Ivy?"

"Yep," he affirmed. "One of the two schools most kids go to around here."

"And it was a boarding school? I mean, you just said whenever you were home from, so I assume you meant when you were on, like, a break?"

Again, she was met with a curt nod. This would be so much easier if she could see his face, yet he was focused forward once more, the hood covering his features. "Yes and no. If you lived close to the schools you could easily remain at home with your family, but considering there are only two Halls of Ivy, those who live further away are granted a room with travel back home over breaks."

Before she could even process the information, he jumped in again. "See the winding building there?"

Sharp bricks of green twisted lazily toward the sky.

"That is the local book shop, Karingons. I've spent more than enough time in there, and if we were to go that way," —he pointed to another sunny road— "we would end up at Simons. They have the best sandwiches. You'll have to try it sometime."

"So... I'll be staying here, or at least near here? Speaking of that, what's the plan after we meet up with your parents. I probably should find a way to contact Althea, considering she's my guardian?"

"One step at a time. My parents have a higher security clearance than me, so they know more. The plan was to get you to them as a safety checkpoint. They can fill you in on everything then."

"Security clearance?" she muttered. Questions kept pinging away at her brain. Things like why did they even want her? Ro often had begrudged the fact that she was a pretty isolated, yet normal girl. She was someone who had never been too far from her hometown and had never done anything too exciting in her life; a plain Jane that most people were able to forget or ignore. It was true she had friends, but usually those she met, no matter if they had an extensive and engagingly long conversation or if it was simple yet quick hello, tended not to remember her the next time they crossed paths. Now though, she was somehow so important that her daily agenda consisted of escaping this group that had been deemed evil, her whole life just tossed upside down without a care. At this point, after every impossible thing she'd seen, you could say the sky was now purple and grass was blue and Ro knew there was a slight chance she might actually believe you. Things were changing; it felt like everything she'd known before had been a lie. The hardest part was everyone—her best friends included—seemed to know more about her than she did.

As they crossed over a small wooden bridge and onto a winding path through the field out of town, Ace must have sensed her hesitation. Slowing, he allowed his voice to gently hang in the air between them. "Can I ask you something, Sparrow? As a friend?"

She slammed the door to her worry and forced her face into a hard smile. "Of course, Aceius. You've answered some of mine."

His shoulder bumped against her own as they walked past the tall blades of grass slanting to the west. "Why aren't you freaking out more?" he asked. "I mean, had I just witnessed half the things you did, I would be losing it, half off my rocker somewhere, but you seem to be handling it okay-ish."

"I honestly don't know." The words felt unsure and heavy on her tongue. "Something about everything you've told me, everything I've seen, just feels right. Although I feel—no, I know—here's more to this whole crazy ordeal than you or anyone else is letting on. My gut knows that I'm on the right path. For instance, I mean, when everything went down with my parents..." The sun shifted, beaming harshly in her eyes. "Waking up in that hospital bed it didn't feel like my memories were suddenly gone, but more like they were stolen. Like someone or something had found a way inside my brain and ripped something from me, leaving nothing in its place but an empty well. I couldn't see past that big gaping wound to remember, but I know in my heart it was something terrible. That there was no way my mom would just suddenly appear and be okay." Ro found herself gulping pack the lump that had lodged itself in her throat.

"Well, no one can say that you aren't strong." Ace squeezed her hand. "And brave. I know many men and women who would have run screaming by now, or checked themselves into a psych ward, but you seem to be doing alright."

Something about the sincerity in his voice eased her rising stress as Ace continued.

"You said that you feel like you are on the right path. Out of curiosity, how did you feel when you were back at home before all of this? Did you still feel like something was off?"

Scrunching her brow, Ro tried to think of a time before all the chaos; a time when there had been a sense of normalcy. But had anything ever truly been normal?

"Yes." Her voice faltered. "And no...? I don't know. There were definite times when things were strange. It's weird. I think that at the time I thought everything was normal, but looking back on it now... I'm not so sure. Especially after everything I've seen." She gestured around them. "I mean, a Vindden is like something out of a fantasy novel, and suddenly you and Adyra are wielding bows and weapons against people who can use... I don't even know what to call it... shadows?... to commit harm... like some weird power... like magic. I feel like I should be in a state of shock and panic, but I'm not... you know? It's like my body is telling me this is normal."

Dirt slid under her feet as she squinted against the glint of a gate up ahead. "After everything I've seen at Althea's and Peri's though? Looking on it now, yeah, maybe something strange was always going on at home. I remember whispered conversations, and my parents arguing a lot with Althea. Though they never said why, I always got the feeling they were arguing about me, or at least something to do with me. Not being allowed to have friends over until Adyra moved next door, and whenever you guys would visit, our parents would spend the first hour or so locked away in Dad's study. In fact, even when Mom gave me this…" Ro raised her arm to show the bracelet dangling off her wrist. "She was really weird about it. Insisting that no matter what, I never take it off. Considering it's a heirloom, I would think she would want me to keep it somewhere safe and only wear it on special occasions, but she almost acted like if I ever take it off, the world would implode."

He nodded at her response. "To her, it might have been the end of the world if you did."

"What do you mean?"

The path took them under the cooling shade of the trees as he answered. "If I remember the story right, your great grandmother once had a piece of jewelry like that commissioned. One that could signal the wearer if they were in contact with those who wished them ill will."

Ro gazed at the wispy chain as it swung with her steps.

"You think this bracelet has some kind of strange power to warn me if I'm in danger?" Remembering the burn from when she hugged Peri, she rubbed her wrist in comfort. "It's just a family heirloom. I'm sure she would have told me if it needed some sort of instruction manual."

His sigh washed over them. "Maybe she couldn't tell you. Maybe she wanted to—needed to—protect you, but couldn't..."

"Beep... Beep.... beeep." He was interrupted by a harsh charm. "Beep.... beep.... Beeeeep.".

Ace stopped, veering them to the right on the walkway. He pulled a vibrating purple compact from his pocket.

"What is that thing?" Ro asked as it shook violently.

He scanned the empty area around them before flipping it open.

"Think of it like a phone," he muttered, mashing a button.

Before Ro could utter a single word, she was met with the high-pitched whine of her best friend. "Where are you two?! You were supposed to check in at Eclipsi, and getting a message through on this thing has been impossible!"

Ace glanced around again before they ducked into the oaks, crouching behind a trunk.

"I tried reaching you, but it was a spotty connection," he said to the device. "You know how it is when the lines are tangled by the distance. Besides, we were on a time crunch, you know this." He rolled his eyes and pushed the hood back, signalling for Ro to do the same.

"Your mouth is moving Aceius, yet all I'm hearing are excuses. Where are you guys, where's Ro?"

He sighed again, more lighthearted this time. "She is fine. We're fine. You know I can't give you our location unless we are on a secure line. Thanks for the concern about me, by the way."

"Yeah yeah, you big baby," the voice squeaked again. "Let me talk to her. I want to see for myself that you two haven't killed each other."

Snorting with amusement, Ace handed the device to a bewildered Ro. "Tell her we're fine, will ya? Just make sure not to give away our plans or location for safety reasons."

Confused, Ro nodded as she turned the device her way.

There, in all her beaming glory, was the grinning bouncing girl. Magenta gleamed off dark locks and brown eyes danced with more than their normal amount of joy. "Yay! You're alive! See, I knew you guys would make it out of that stupid SUV! Ugh, that was such a problem. Anyway, hi darling, how are you?" Every word was practically sung. "Is Ace being nice? Or, well, scratch that. Are *you* being nice to him? Oh, OH, have you…? Wait, can't ask that." Her face scrunched off in concentration before brightening once more, and Ro wondered how she found time to breathe. "Are you going to say anything or continue to stand there all wide-eyed and slack jawed?"

Snapping herself back to the present, Ro shook her head free of questions. The device seemed to act like a phone; yet, as she stared at it in her hands, she saw Adyra's grinning face shooting from the screen in a hologram, as if a mini version of her was there with them—a futuristic video chat, the likes of which Ro had only ever seen in sci-fi movies.

"Adyra?" she asked the device, only to be met with a fierce chuckle.

"Yep, the one and only. Sorry I forgot you wouldn't know what a koble was. This stuff kind of takes getting used to, I guess, but it's really cool and helpful."

"Ko-ble," Ro mouthed, shooting a glance at her grinning companion. "Um, yeah sorry, you, this, well, the whole situation just kinda threw me off a bit, I guess. Can you see me like I can see you?"

"Yep! Just the same. A teeny-tiny version of you standing in front of me. So cute! I can also hear Ace's annoying snickering near you as well. Like I said, nice to see you two haven't torn each other to bits."

"Not for lack of trying." Ro let a smile slip past her tired façade. "Where are you? I thought you were supposed to meet us at Eclipsi."

"Again, not a secure line," Ace groaned.

"He's right, I can't really tell you. I did, though, have a minute to slip away and try to contact you guys again."

"Again?" Ro asked, confused.

"Yeah." Adyra rolled her eyes. "I've been trying off and on all day, but with the lines being tangled, I couldn't get through."

"Tangled lines?"

"Yep again, my little mimic."

"You're starting to sound like a parrot, Sparrow,"

Ace chipped in as he ruffled through his pack.

"There was a big outage all over last night," Adyra explained. "Now the lines are acting funky and making it nearly impossible to get a call through. Think of it like a phone line being down, but in this case all of them are, oh, and they're invisible."

"That sounds… complicated."

Adyra's face turned grave. "It is, but you're okay, right? Like, you're doing okay? I know this can really take a dig at one's mental health."

"Yeah, yeah, I'm alright. We're…" Ace sent her a hurried look, face screaming not to give any details that could compromise their location. "We're both alright. You? Did you get away from Peri's okay?"

"I'm alive, and I'm glad you two are as well!"

A deep voice shouted in the background, causing the bow-carrying girl's face to fall flat, void of emotion.

"Listen, Ro, I have to go, but I'll see you soon, okay? Stay close to Ace, he practically wrote this plan. Could you pass the koble to him now?"

A commotion boomed through the connection and Adyra's head shot to the left, staring at something on her end that Ro could not see. The sudden stiffness in her tone worried Ro past any attempts to argue.

"Sure, be safe," she said, setting the koble into her companion's outstretched hand.

Even though they were the only ones on or near the path, Ro still felt like she was being watched as she lifted the hood to cover her face once more. The sun signalled its descent as the moon chillingly greeted it. How long had it been since her birthday? Families would be eating dinner and getting ready for bed as they prepared for the next day. Yet here she was in some unknown place, unsure of what was to come. Shivering as the cool breeze drifted past, she found herself tuning back into her friend's conversation.

"It's broken, Ace, it's been broken for a while now. We're trying the best we can. I've got my top members in the forefront, but if you don't hurry, I don't know if we can keep this up much longer."

"Stick to the plan," Ace said. "With the koble lines messing up there is no way we can contact everyone to get changes cleared or acknowledged."

"Respectfully, I think this is getting too risky and you're being stubborn, but I see your logic," the girl all but grumbled. "We will proceed on our end and I'll meet you guys soon."

At this, Ace put his own hood on before scanning the area once more. "See you there, Adyra. Thanks for the update." He went to close the device before she chirped out one last thing.

"Oh, and Ace…" Her voice became a bit thicker. "Stay safe, okay?"

Ro watched as he crooked a smile. "Always." With that, he flipped the koble shut, slipping it back in a hidden pocket once more.

"You ready?" His gaze blazed Ro's way.

"Ready as I'll ever be." She smiled once more as they stepped onto the path again. "You don't think…?" She paused, watching as his hand rested where she knew his sword would be. "You don't think the Nefarie are following us do you, or that they've found Adyra?"

She watched as his form hardened into stone. "They are on our trail in some way I suppose, but as for around us right now? No, I wouldn't say they're even close."

"Careful," she found herself laughing at the darkness of it all. "You'll jinx us with confidence like that."

At her giggle, his features softened. "What can I say? If we fear them then we are already losing by giving them what they want"

CHAPTER NINE

ce's words echoed through her as she examined his face in the fading light. How was he not wearier? Or Adyra? How was she so cheerful when they talked earlier? Other than the weird sign off, she seemed totally normal, as happy as ever.

Ace broke the silence as they rounded over a hill "We're almost there," he said.

Through the gleaming rays of the setting sun, a dark bronze gate clashed with the purple hues of the sky. To the left, a small brick driveway deviated from the main road.

The entrance sat open in the distance, welcoming them to the looming house beyond.

"This is where you grew up?" Ro asked.

"Technically speaking, yes. The estate has always been in my family. Don't give me that look either." He let out a high-pitched snort. "It's technically my great grandfather's house, I just grew up here until I was old enough to leave for school."

"What look?" Ro tossed her hands up with a smile, "I just never knew you lived in a mansion."

"It's not a—" His eyes rolled upwards as he walked on, scoffing. "Come on, never mind." Gesturing for her to follow him, he led the way. To her surprise, he didn't go down the driveway, but to the left of the fence just alongside the tree line.

"I thought we were going to see your parents," Ro asked cautiously "Don't we, you know, need to actually go inside to do that?"

As they passed the house, Ace pulled her from the view of a back porch. "Yes, but before that, I need to make sure the area hasn't been compromised." He spoke to her in a hushed manner.

"Why are you whispering?"

"There was a car in front, one I didn't recognize."

Ro moved to peer toward the stone building before she felt herself suddenly yanked back.

"What are you doing?" Ace scolded. "Don't look!"

"Okay okay, sorry! Couldn't your parents just have, like, visitors or something?"

"Not right now. They didn't know exactly when we were coming, but they would have been prepared by making sure the house was safe from the Nefarie. That does not include visitors."

"It could be just a neighbour stopping by. Adyra said that the lines were down. Maybe your mom was worried and they called a friend for back up or something."

"True," he said, observing the area again, his face stiff. "Still, I would prefer to check the house anyway. Just stay here. I'll be right back"

"This is ridiculous; we're safer together."

"No, you're safer away from any potential danger, okay?" His tone softened as he looked at her. "This one time, don't fight me on this, please. It's my job to make sure you're safe; besides, Adyra would kill me if I let you walk in there all willy-nilly."

The worry creasing his brow convinced her not to argue. If going in alone first then coming out to get her made everyone feel better, then fine. "Okay, for the record though, I want it noted that I still think this is a stupid idea. Every horror movie fan knows the golden rule: never ever split up!"

"Thank you." he said, relief flooding his tone as he thrust the koble into her hands. "Keep this. If any-thing—and I mean anything—seems off, there is a small river dead ahead. I want you to run in that direction and follow it until you reach Doven again. Don't look back or wait for me."

"I'm not just going to leave you." Her tone cracked with exasperation.

"I'll be fine," he stressed before moving to leave. "If I am not back in twenty minutes, use the koble to call Adyra after you're safe in Doven. She'll send a scout party for you."

"Wait, Ace! What if I can't reach Adyra? Even If I

do, what do I tell her?"

"Then you keep trying. She will know what to do."

"Wait, Aceius!" she whisper-yelled as he disappeared back the way they had come.

This was ludicrous. The tired girl slumped against the rough tree bark. She had agreed to stay put but still didn't think it was the wisest idea. It had to be better than painting a target on their backs by starting an argument in the middle of the woods though, so she had conceded. That didn't stop her running thoughts from reminding her of every horror movie that had the trope of killing off the separated party members fist—bonus points for the ones she remembered that took place at night. Refusing to admit that the stereotypical childhood fear of the dark pricked at the back of her mind, Ro focused on her annoyance instead as she sat between some prickly bushes, tall oaks shrouding her from the rising moon,

The silence allowed her mind to relax, drifting back to that dream once more. Although it had felt more like a memory, every detail was still there, no foggy remains of a disillusioned REM session. It had felt, and still did feel, like she had been truly there watching those two people beside the river that night. Their voices echoed in her head.

"The girl is smart, yet she's clueless about who she really is. We still have our resources; we still can win this battle."

It haunted her. Who was the girl they were talking of? Could it be her? And if so, she wasn't so clueless anymore. At first, Ro had just tossed it aside, another weird dream. Yet something Ace had said stuck with her. "They call themselves the Nefarie."

At the time of having the dream she had never even heard a mention of their name, let alone knew anything about the shadowed group. How could she have had a dream about them without ever having known of them? Maybe she was remembering things wrong, but that particular moment in the dream had been very vivid. Almost too lifelike to be something her subconscious made up.

A shiver raced over her. When the time was right, Ro decided she would bring up the dream to Ace; in all honesty, she didn't know why she hadn't approached the subject before. Something in her had held her back from sharing those details, a feeling in her gut scream-ing for her to keep silent. Maybe after all this trouble she was being a little too cautious, just a bit untrusting. It wasn't that she didn't trust her friends, thinking about it further she realized that she had completely forgiven them at this point. If what they said was true — and everything she had seen pointed to that fact — then they hadn't abandoned her after all, but instead were only trying to help in what ways they could. Honestly, at this point the only reasonable explanation she could think of for the strange occurrences she had experi-enced was that she had never woken up at the hospital. Maybe she was in some long coma, or some weird ver-sion of a spirit journey she accidentally tripped upon. She knew deep down that wasn't true though, there was much more going on than she realized. Either way, Ro prepared herself for the warm heat of embarrassment, because as soon as she saw Ace's family, her questions would come tumbling out in a tangled word vomit and she expected some real answers this time.

Soon it would be fully dark. The crisp air started to creep through her clothes and the ground grew damp. Her fingertips grew stiff against the cold koble she held. Ace said twenty minutes, but she realized in that moment that she had no way of telling the time exactly. It couldn't have been more than that though, she thought.

Ro eased her back away from the scratchy bark of the tree and surveyed the area, hoping to hear his approach or a signal that it was okay to come toward the house. The calm she felt slowly dispersed. What if something had happened and she had no clue? What if she had just been a sitting duck for her unknown attackers? Birds had long ago stopped their soft songs and the forest was setting down for the night when a small animal sprinted past her, sliding on the fallen leaves as it raced into a bush, causing Ro to launch from her position into a stiff crouch of surprise.

Ace had asked her to stay where she was, insinuating she would be safe there, yet it felt like he had been gone too long. The soft glow of a light from the back of the house reached into the trees and the worry she was trying to gulp down threatened to override her normally reasonable brain. Ro was alert, hyper aware in the blowing wind. Her tired legs protested as she cautiously raised herself to stand. After all this pressure on them she was going to need a long hot bath to relive the ache of her muscles; if she survived this weird and terrifying journey that is.

Groaning as her back cracked, Ro glanced around the large tree that felt like her safety line. Surely she would have heard some indication that things had gone wrong by now. In her limited experience, the Nefarie brought nothing but chaos and explosions. She shuddered again at the remembrance of the glittering, heavy smoke they seemed to wield as a weapon. She knew Ace had said if he wasn't back in twenty minutes to run but Ro didn't want to just leave him; besides, she told herself as an excuse, with the sun setting she was worried of getting lost in the thick of the woods. What if she ran only to draw more attention to herself on a silent evening like this? At this thought, the area around her felt more unsafe, her eyes darting to every darkened corner, praying she wouldn't make out a hidden face.

The house had to be the lesser evil at this point, and her increasing panic convinced her it couldn't hurt to look and see if there was any trouble. Ace was probably walking toward her right now and she could always meet him halfway.

She wouldn't leave the woods and enter the property, Ro told herself. She'd just take a look. For all she knew, he was caught up with whatever company his parents had. The remaining sensible part of her brain told her this wasn't correct. Ace wouldn't leave her sitting alone and scared in the cold woods, but she was too far convinced by the panic inside to listen to reason.

Wind hit her widened eyes as they fixed on that shimmering light of the house in the distance. Ro slowly began to move forward, trying her hardest to step not only slowly but as lightly as possible. If anyone was out there, she didn't want to alert them by snapping a twig or tripping on a vine. Ducking around some low hanging limbs and teetering over plants, Ro found herself looking frantically for any sign of Ace's towering figure, but she was only greeted by a dark empty forest.

The feeling of someone watching her settled into her spine. If she could just keep moving forward, then she felt like she would be just fine. A twig snapped to her left, disrupting the eerie silence that had become the soundtrack to her current adventure. Whipping around, Ro realized she could no longer make out much on that side but the dark shadows of trees. Stumbling backwards, she turned and ran for the edge of the property as fast as she could, the house light being her only guidance through the worry.

Weaving through trees, she begged for it to have just been a harmless animal, not some horrid being out to get her. Seeing some leafy bushes just ahead, Ro found herself tripping, sliding into them, hidden yet able to see the house perfectly. She scanned the area for any sign of her friend as her heart hammered. Why did she think it was a smart idea to leave her small area of safety? She should have just stayed put or ran to the river like they had spoken about. What if something really was wrong, or that twig snapping had been someone from the Nefarie? Yet she knew she still wouldn't have run for Doven; she wouldn't leave her friend behind.

Ro squeezed her eyes shut and focused on slowing her erratic breathing to a point where she couldn't be heard. Did they see her hide in the bush? Were they waiting just outside, laughing and holding their attack until she made her cramped position known? Ro forced herself to open her eyes, peering between the small leafy limbs that covered her. Looking for the stoic stance of a cloaked Nefarie or the menacing chuckle of the raspy-voiced guy who had chased her from Althea's to Peri's. She saw nothing but the forest on one side and the house and yard on the other. No one was coming to attack her.

But how much longer could she really stay here, hidden in the massive cloak? Cursing herself for leaving her previous spot, Ro realized that when Ace came back, she wouldn't be where he expected to find her. If she wasn't careful, she might just miss him coming all together. Taking a few deep breaths for courage, Ro came to a decision; after all, hadn't he said that giving into the fear was letting them win? Doing a quick check behind her to make sure there was no thick black fog of the Nefarie to consume her, she forced herself to be brave and slowly stood up, hood hiding her face, to walk toward the light she could see illuminating from a back porch.

This was either the dumbest thing she had done or the smartest, but with every step she took, Ro felt herself getting braver and angrier. Sure, Ace wouldn't be happy with her, but best case scenario, everything was okay. And worst case scenario: the so called Nefarie would get a piece of her mind, or she would go down fighting. Whatever happened in this house, she would weather it with Ace as soon as she found him.

Still creeping slowly as to not make much noise, Ro could make out some sort of commotion through the windows of the brightly lit mansion. Not loud enough to disrupt the evening of a passerby, but there were shadows of figures madly gesturing, arms flying frantically around in white hot anger.

"Done! I can't believe you!" Ace's hardened voice met her ears, muffled by the thick walls.

Stopping in confusion, Ro strained to listen further. Though his voice was difficult to make out, there was a cold edge she had only heard once before, during the attack at Peri's. It held a hardness that made him sound almost inhuman.

Stunned, she flinched as the back door swung open violently, and she blinked back the pain of the sudden bright light. The figure in the doorway materialized in front of her adjusting vision and a silence came over the property once more. It was a tense quiet that his shocked whisper sliced through like a searing knife. "What are you doing?" he hissed at her.

"Aceius!" A sharp bark came from in the house. "This conversation is not over!"

His eyes doubled in size as he shared a look with her. A look most might see as angry and determined but she could make out his blue rimmed pupils flash with fear.

With a sudden slam that shook the windows of the whole first floor, he came running at her.

"What? I know you said—" she began, but he grabbed her hand, pulling away from the house.

"Run!" he ordered, sounding much like his father who had shouted before. His long strides did most of the work, pulling her back into that hated forest as she heard the door burst open once more.

"Aceius, wait! Please, you don't understand." His mother's voice rang tearfully into the night.

"What—?" Ro gasped for air as he continued to pull her along. "What happened?" She stumbled, catching herself from falling as he continued to pull on her arm.

"Twenty minutes," he all but growled, turning as they reached the river. "Twenty minutes and you agreed to run for Doven."

"Ace, slow down! Your legs are longer than mine! I can barely keep up, and I wasn't just going to leave you. Besides, I didn't know which way to go when I reached the river and it was getting too dark."

Behind them, thundering feet crashed through the underbrush of the forest they had just been in.

A deep voice echoed in the night. "Son, make this easy on all of us here. Make the right choice for you and Ro."

"If we slow down, they catch up," Ace said. "Keep running, Sparrow!"

They rounded a curve and were back in the forest again.

"I'm not stupid," Ace said, his voice biting through

the cold night. "I knew you wouldn't really leave me there no matter how much I asked you to, but I at least thought you would stay in the safety of the spot I had left you at so that you could be found if something happened to me, but of course you just had to go see the excitement for yourself."

Ro's stomach felt sick and twisted as they flew down a hill into a part of the woods darker and more densely overgrown. "Don't be angry just because I didn't have the heart to leave you behind!" she fought back.

Ace huffed. "I have the military training to—"

"I don't care!" she interrupted, hair flying wildly as it embraced the freedom from her fallen hood. "You are my friend, Ace. I wasn't going to—and never will—leave you behind!"

His features remained hard, but she felt him squeeze her hand just a little bit tighter.

"What happened?" she gasped again as her legs cried out for relief.

"The area was compromised," he told her, his voice heavy with anger.

"But your parents?"

His face grew dark as they pushed on against the soundtrack of a raging army. "They're not who I thought they were."

CHAPTER TEN

hey ran until Ro was sure she would collapse from exhaustion. The sound of people chasing them turned in a different direction.

"We stop here," Ace announced, his feet skidding as he halted their escape. They stood amid a meagre clearing where large fir trees jutted upwards from the damp ground, surrounding them.

He dropped her hand, pulling a closed fist from his pocket. With impossible speed he slammed his hands to a clap, crying into the wind, *Ventus tuere nos ab hoste habitum!*"

Glittering mist shot outwards, swirling its way to the edge of the clearing and upwards, forming a magenta wall at the edge of their small meadow and jabbing at the sky before dissipating.

"What the hell was that?" Ro shouted, backing away.

Ace stood, more relaxed now, an ease flowing from him as he surveyed the area providing them refuge. "A cloaking charm to hide us from them," he said calmly.

"Because that massive show wasn't obvious enough for you?"

Ace sighed as he turned, bending long limbs to gather twigs and brush into a circle between them. "No one but us could see it, and as long as you don't cross the edges of this clearing, no one can find you; same with me." He sat down, gesturing next to him. "Now come on, the sun is gone."

"No."

"No?" His eyes gleamed with amusement. "No to the spell, or no to sitting down, or no to the fact that it's nighttime? Because I don't know if you've looked around, Ro, but it's gotten pretty dark."

It irritated her that he was right as she spared a darting glance toward the amber slithering below blackened clouds above. "No as in I am not cooperating with you any further until you tell me what's going on. How do we know they are not still chasing us?"

He lowered one palm to the ground and closed his eyes. A fire suddenly blazed, heat blasting into her face before settling down into a smoky crackle. Light reflected off his smirk as he arched an eyebrow her way. "They will continue to search for a bit, but they can't find us unless we leave this clearing. To anyone on the outside, it looks empty, and the charm dissuades their subconscious from wanting to enter. Besides... this has been you cooperating?" He chuckled.

"Yes, I mean… well, as cooperative as I can be regarding the situation. Before this—" she gestured to the space between them— "goes any further, I need an explanation. A full explanation. And I mean everything, not just tidbits like you gave me before. Like how you just lit that fire for example?" "

He sighed as he motioned beside him again. "I wasn't supposed to tell you, but considering the circumstances, you deserve that much. Sit down."

Despite everything, Ro still trusted him. She lowered herself to the ground beside him, accepting the heat from the suspicious flames.

"Where should we start?" he asked, eyes blazing.

After all this secrecy, he was going to fill her in now? Giving in just like that? Sure, he had told her a little tale at Eclipsi, but was he finally offering her all the answers? Ro realized that here, in the dark of this strange place, she was finally ready to speak the impossible. "Magic is…" Her mind raced around the very idea. "Magic is real.

"Yes." A smile cut across his tired features, and for a moment she swore she saw what resembled the person she knew.

"It's very real," he continued. "You have seen it. At Peri's, on Claudaith. It's how we got here. I went over this a bit already…"

"I know. It's just… magic is real," she repeated with wide eyes. "And that was a cloaking spell?"

"Yes." "His eyes danced mischievously again as Ro leaned toward him. "Basically, I called upon the wind to hide us. It's a simple charm you learn in school."

"The wind is a mindless thing; how can it help you?"

He sighed again; a sigh not laden with irritation, but with a gentle exhaustion as he turned toward her. "You want the whole story? Like magic, why you're here and were never told of it, the whole shebang?"

"Well, duh." Ro shoved his arm lightly, forgetting for a moment the heaviness of the past few days. "Everything!"

"Okay, okay, but you have to listen. Like actually listen. It's a long story."

Flames illuminated his face as Ace looked her in the eyes, finally willing to tell her what he knew.

"Right now, we are still technically in Eclipsi, just another part of the forest, the southern region in fact." The casualness of longtime friendship enveloped them. "Closer toward Merwin."

"Merwin?"

"It's one of the two main kingdoms here, where the Fae courts reside."

"Fae? As in Fairies? With wings and granting wishes? Like Peter Pan faeries?"

His snort interrupted the peace. "That's stereotypical. The wings I understand because the use of wind for flight, but granting wishes I'll never get. It's not like we're fluttering versions of Tinkerbell."

The imagery was enough to make her giggle. "Well, it would be a funny sight. So you're a faerie? This is unreal"

"Yes, I am Fae, but we tend not to use the word Faerie too often, though those in the mortal realm like it a lot."

"The mortal realm? Like Claudaith and Aylee?" She found herself curiously questioning everything he said. Magic was one thing, but being in a place that didn't exist on any map she had ever seen was another. The breeze picked up, dancing in between the flames and casting shadows in the darkness.

Ro tossed him a grateful grin as he shrugged off his cloak, laying it over her to use against the cold. "Thank you," she said.

He just nodded before turning his gaze to the fire as he began.

"The mortal realm, I'm sure you've gathered, is where we were before we left the great tree at Eclipsi. Think of the Vindden like a door to another realm or dimension, where nothing is geographically different, but everything else has changed. It's where you were born, and where your parents fled to a long time ago."

This was news to her: her parents fleeing. They had never disclosed how they met, just that they were both on their own when they found each other and formed a family. As far as she knew, her parents were quiet, small-town people. They didn't like to make a fuss of stories from the past, so they had simply never been told. Ro groaned internally. How silly of her it was to not wonder about their past.

"So, if we're not in the normal realm where earth is then… then we're…?"

"Mageia," he said. "We are currently in the realm of Mageia.

Then his incredible story truly began.

"A long time ago, many many eons past the time of most mortal's remembrance, there was only one realm. What is now the mortal realm was home to both humans and the supernatural alike, and there was a great peace as the system between the three kingdoms worked for all."

"Three kingdoms?" her words seemed to tiptoe out. "That doesn't make any sense, even in the time of kings and queens there would have been multiple kingdoms spanning across the continents."

"You have to think before even that, Ro." He smiled. "Sure, there were multiple mortal courts and villages with a certain hierarchy, but at this given time, for many centuries, there was only one ruling king of the mortals, and he worked together with the other two kingdoms to form an alliance throughout the land. You had the house of mortals, sure; but then, alongside them was the house of Elves and the court of Fae. The mortals, the Fae, and the Elves lived harmoniously, working together to form relationships and bonds that lasted lifetimes, but once the Scindo started there was no turning back."

The crackling heat warmed her face, and as Ro listened, she imagined she see the story play out in the dancing flames.

"There had always been wars and fights between the mortal lands. Originally, anyone with magical blood avoided the conflict, choosing instead to stick to our way of life and the belief that magic cannot—and should not—be used for others' pain.

"That was until the Scindo. The Human King, Edric's son, turned against him and his peaceful rulings, causing bloodshed and pain. He was a chaotic, crazed man, fighting to be leader, who didn't care how many mortals lost their lives. King Edric turned to the Fae and Elven leaders, desperate for assistance to return the land to its normal peaceful ways. With innocent lives being lost and the destruction increasing, for the first time ever those with magical blood were permitted to join the fights. We sent in healers, warriors like the praesidium, those who could help raise the numbers of the living and defeat the demented prince."

"So, with you joining the war, the king won?" Ro guessed, enamoured by the tale.

"Yes and no." Ace smiled sadly. "The king was poisoned by an assassin, left to die a slow agonizing death. The next night, after he exhaled his last ragged breath, the prince lay defeated on the battlefield, and the rest rode to victory. Both father and son died within hours of each other, both losing claim to the throne and the land." Shadows danced as he spoke, smoke curling its way upward in the night sky.

"And that was the Scindo?" Ro wondered.

He shook his head. "No. That was the battle leading up to the Scindo. You see, humankind had never seen the full extent of magic, until this battle that is. Besides the normal healing spells, they saw the damage that magic could do if wielded by the wrong hands; and like most people when faced with something they do not understand, they began to grow fearful of those with magical blood. Edric's brother took over as king and elected a high court to determine the depths of magic and how they could possibly gain it for their own use."

"Magical blood is only in the Elves and Fae?" A chill had picked up, carrying her words to him slowly.

"Sort of, yes."

She tightened his cloak against the wind.

"There are many magical creatures: Bakru, Dryads, and fire-birds to name a few. They have limited magical abilities and are not as conscious of it as Elves and Fae. At this time, they all lived in what would be the mortal realm. But it was the Elven and Fae magic that mortals had witnessed, and the new king wanted to harvest. Unfortunately for them, it doesn't work that way. The only way one can have magical abilities is through genetics. Magic is in one's blood and tethered with one's life-force. If you don't have magic when you are born, then you won't ever have magic. Humans realized this, but not until the new king had lost many attempts to obtain it for himself. So humankind grew weary, and the new king grew mad. He spread propaganda until all with magical blood were not only hated but feared by the public. That's when the Scindo began."

"Propaganda? Like rumours?"

"Yeah." His face scrunched with disgust. "It doesn't take long to fear something you don't understand, and after the great war, the humans were shaken and scared. It didn't take much for them to turn their backs on the relationships and ties they had built with the Elven and Fae."

Trees began to sway in the background, chorusing his tale. "Soon," he continued, "it became unsafe for anyone with magical blood to leave their kingdoms. Traps were set and human assassins were sent out to kill innocent and unknowing targets. The Elven court of the time and Fae king fought to realign the peace there had once been, but the new mortal king had gone too far and shaken humankind to the very core. The bonds that had once been were severed, and the magical kind began to be unsafe even in their homes as mortals started to hunt them down. Being a kind and gentle man, the Fae king ordered all magical beings not to use magic against the humans, since it was what scared them the most; but as time went on, things got worse, and the Magical kind grew smaller and smaller and lost more and more to the reckless bloodshed. The human king demanded magic and refused to understand that for a man of mortal blood like him, it was impossible. Once they found out about the testing on those with magical blood being done, the Fae and Elven courts joined forces to work day in and out, protecting their people whilst losing all hope of resuming normalcy with humans. The losses grew and it soon became obvious there was no turning back. Unless the mortal king received magical abilities of his own, we might have gone extinct. Snuffed out like a light."

"And the human king couldn't have magic because he wasn't genetically born with it?" The idea of someone so cruel struck her. "Couldn't someone just explain this to him?"

"He was beyond reason, and at this point led humankind to slaughtering all those who showed a sign of magic. He earned himself the name the Crimson Czar."

"So," Ro piped in again, her heart aching for so much loss, "what happened to these people?"

"Well," he sighed, "it became imperative to save the magical kind at any cost, yet the Fae king still hoped for some peace. It soon became obvious that the humans were convinced that the only way to be safe was to end magic once and for all. At the time, there was a young Fae prince, Breenus, who was just ending his studies at the Halls of Ivy. He wondered if there was a way to end the Scindo on both sides, permanently. Soon his idea was presented at the house of Rymi."

"Rymi?" Half of what he was saying felt foreign and uncomfortable on her tongue; she felt like she had somehow fallen into a fantasy movie

"I believe you would call them physical cosmologist's now. Scientists who study not only space and time, but the dynamics of the universe. Breenus was curious to discover if he could combine their knowledge to create another place, one much safer, for all magical creatures to live in peace."

"So, another realm? Like this one or…?"

"Yeah, exactly like this one. Breenus worked together with the Rymi for over a year as the Scindo raged on, testing out ideas and possibilities. Finally, he came to a solution. Only it had one massive problem.

Using that much magic—that much power—could be more dangerous and unstable than one mere Fae or Elf could withstand."

Ro's face scrunched up in confusion. "But if he had magic, isn't it like renewable or something? Like an unlimited supply? And why did he have to do it on his own?"

"He wasn't on his own, but only one person could cast the spell needed and it required a lot of power—more than one Elf or Fae would have on their own. You're right though, magic is renewable and in a way, you are born with an unlimited supply because magic is a part of who you are as a person. It is tethered to your life-force, but because of that it is very draining, especially if you use it without practice. Over time, through training and schoolwork, simple charms and spells, even advanced magic in your specialized element, tend not to be so tiring or harmful to one's health, but this spell was something no one had ever seen or come close to doing before as it required all elemental uses of magic."

Ro found herself entranced.

"Most Elves and Fae are born with a preference toward a certain type of magic. They tend to be better, stronger even, at earth, fire, water, or wind magic specifically. Sometimes, with practice and the right genetic history, they can even use two that go hand in hand—like fire with earth or water with wind—but only a few times in history has one been born with the ability to use all types of magic with the help of an

Iahde, someone who is a source."

"A source for the magic?"

"Sort of. An Iahde is someone who has the ability to allow the magic to flow through them, almost like a fountain allowing it to course into another. But those who can access magic this way are rare. In fact, there are only two records of an Omnes magicae and an Iahde being born before."

"Omnes magicae?" Again, the words rested unnaturally on her tongue.

"The one who can pull strength from the land and use the magic accessed by the Iahde. It is very draining and dangerous for both though, as using all forms of magic can turn disastrous and eat at your life-force. All records of an Omnes magicae and Iahde have ended in disaster."

"What kind of disaster?" she dared to ask.

"Pain and death," he responded. "And it just so happened that Breenus and his wife, Elsina, were Omnes magicae and Iahde themselves."

"So, they could use any type of magic?" she asked, immersed in the history as the flames leapt higher.

"And they did," Ace replied gravely. "After multiple trial and error experiments, Breenus, Elsina, and the Rymi came to the realization that the necessary spell could only be cast by one, while the others created protection and support charms for the caster and all magical creatures alike."

Ro felt like she could see it. A group of people huddled over books in a dank library, hoping to find a solution. Stress and tension heavy in the air as they flipped through multiple pages.

"As the history teachers tell us, on a dark night when the wind screamed and the sky cried for the destruction of all, the Rymi escorted both Breenus and Elsina to the highest cliff beside a turbulent sea, and with the permission of both the Fae king and Elvin high courts, they cast their spell. The Rymi joined hands, as the praesidium fought to keep off approaching human forces. They began their chants to protect the young couple and all magical kind alike. Holding tight to their bond, Breenus cast the potion they had created into the waters below, shifting the dark blue waves to a churning amber ocean. Elsina allowed all elemental magic to course through her, channelling to him as he cried to the angry sky, twisting and forming the dimension and changing the land.

"Breenus shouted until his voice grew hoarse. They say the couple spent five agonizing hours until finally, a gateway appeared: a shimmering hole torn right off the cliff itself. All magical creatures, including those of Fae and Elvin blood, were rushed through this new portal. A set of warriors came first as no one knew what to expect, joined soon by the people carrying the supernatural creatures along with them, to be released in the wild at their new destination. After that, both high courts followed, the Fae king refusing the leave without his son. They rushed through the praesidium and the Rymi. The humans were fast approaching though, and with no one left to fight, the young couple knew they had to proceed fast. With the last of his energy spent, Breenus leapt off the cliff, pulling Elsina along with him.

"They both were weak, the spell draining and pulling from both their life-forces, taking a price higher than most would be willing to pay; yet as they jumped through together, Elsina summed up just enough magic for one final spell in the mortal world, a gift of final goodbyes. She knew it wasn't the human's fault that they were propelled by fear and led by tyranny. Against the tears in her eyes, she looked at the home she was disappearing from and cast a spell to cause all left in the land to forget magic ever existed. Although some memory must have stayed in humankind's subconscious because you still have fairy tales and the like."

Ro's eyes hung heavy now, saddened for all the people in the tale who had been forced out of their homes, and even though Ace's story had seemed outlandish, something told her it was right. She could feel that he was telling the truth. Ro thought back to the magic she had witnessed so far. "So they came to this place?"

"Yes, when they arrived the people realized they were in a land much like the one they had just left. The same mountains and valleys, the same coasts and rivers, all in the same places, just untouched by mankind. So they settled down and made a home here. This became Magica, and that became the mortal realm. The Elven high court formed the Skye Kingdom and the Fae made home in the Kingdom of Merwin, with both living in the villages and towns throughout this land. That's when they created the Vindden just in case we ever needed to go back. The original tree sits below the waves of that cliff, forever tying the worlds together."

"And what happened to everyone else? The Fae king? Breenus and Elsina?"

"After it was all said and done, both Elves and Fae agreed on one thing, the saviours that had brought them to this new land should be the ones to lead it. Although both had claims to the throne, at the time the Fae king happily stepped down and let his son and daughter-in-law become the rulers to this new kingdom."

"And let me guess," Ro laughed. "They lived happily ever after?"

His smile dropped quicker than she expected. "Not exactly. The price of the spells they used was too high. It drained Breenus' life-force too much, aging him drastically and causing a weakness he could never recover from." He sighed. "Most with magic in their blood live to be thousands of years old, as the ageing process is progressively slower after your 19th birthday when you reach your full power potential, but King Breenus died no less than two years later, at the age of 992, leaving his queen to rule without him."

"That's sad," Ro muttered, feeling for the loss of so many. "But still, 992—that's a long life."

"By your standards." He smiled again.

"So then there was peace?"

"Yes… and no. During the Scindo, a small yet radical group began to form, at first protesting the inability to defend themselves with magic, then arguing that humankind should be the ones hunted down and stomped out. Honestly, I think they started out with good intentions but led themselves down a dark path. They refused leaving, protesting that magical lives were far superior to mortals, and they believed we should have taken over that realm, ruling it completely."

Cold chills sent shivers down her spine, and Ro could swear she felt stares from the forest's shadows once more. Bringing her knees to her chest, it all began to make sense. The darkness following her, the voice as she hid behind the dresser, the attack at Peri's house. Everything was clicking into place and it terrified her. "It's the Nefarie, isn't it?" The words slipped out unintentionally, almost as if speaking them would bring the very haunts here themselves.

His curt nod was enough to make her glance to the shadows once more. Could they be watching from afar like they were at Althea's?

Almost as if he could read her mind, Ace placed his hand on her arm gently. "Anyone who was not inside the cloaking spell when I cast it would not be able to find us. You're safe, Ro."

The simple words did not alleviated her fears, but they did cast a small shimmer of relief through the waterfall of her anxiety. "Why are they after me, Ace? What did I ever do to them? It's not like I even knew about any of this."

"It's not what you did, it's what you are."

Her head snapped to attention at his words. "Who I am?"

The leaves of a nearby oak danced as something came flying downwards. Denting the wet grass in front of them, two booted feet appeared. A half hood covered lavender hair as a young woman greeted them. With a devilish grin and a purring voice she called out. "Hello, cousin."

CHAPTER ELEVEN

ce launched to his feet, placing himself in between the two girls. Ro leapt to join him. No longer tired, she watched his figure stiffen, pointing his claymore toward the figure's widening grin.

"Threatening me with your sword, Aceius?" she said, chuckling. "Now come on, I thought we were family. That's kinda rude, don't cha think?"

His steel words cut through her sass. "How did you get past the cloaking spell, Zee?" His voice was cold, hard even, the dark edge back again, causing Ro to look on cautiously. Stepping out past his extended left arm, she got a closer glimpse at the person Ace currently held as a threat.

Lavender skin crinkled in joy at the edges of the girl's vibrant iridescent eyes. "Oh, calm down, cousin." She waved her hands as if brushing a bit of dust away.

"I was already in the space of your cloaking charm before you cast it. After all this time, I just wanted to meet your family's famed little bird."

Ro could have sworn she heard Ace curse out under his breath.

"Leave now, Zee, I don't want to hurt you."

Despite the way he seemed to perceive this girl as a threat, her resounding giggle was enough to make Ro come forward. *Is this foolish?* she wondered, but she was tired of letting others defend her."

Ace shot her a glare that would have frozen another in their tracks, but Ro just rolled her eyes and tried to push past him. Grabbing her wrist, he muttered, "Stay back, I can't defend you if you're putting yourself at risk."

"And I," she emphasized, "am not some damsel in distress."

Laughter bubbled out from Zee as she stood in front of them. "Ace, just let her meet me. I'm seriously no threat, test me! Brianna gave her the bracelet for that reason."

Ro shot a glance toward the charm on her wrist. "You…" She paused. "You know my mother?"

"No, sorry," the mysterious girl's face softened. "Living with Ace, I caught a few things, that's all. But I heard she's an amazing woman."

Remembering how her arm had burned at Peri's, Ro decided there was no time as good as the present to try out the heirloom. "Fine," she said, taking a tentative step forward. "Keep the sword up, Ace." She gulped down a lump of nerves. "If this will tell us whether she can be trusted, then what better way to put it to the test?"

"Ro!" Ace sputtered, worry crinkling his face. "Don't."

Ro knew her smile looked as rocky as she felt. "I've got you if anything happens, right?" She turned and extended her hand toward the stranger. "Sparrow."

"Zeendria," the girl chirped in reply as their hands clasped into a shake.

Ro shot her eyes to the jewelled charm, waiting for the intense burn, that jolt that would tell her Zeendria was evil, a part of the Nefarie. Nothing happened. The cool metal lay dormant, glittering in the moonlight.

"Seeeeeee?" Zee called out happily. "Not a bad guy."

A reluctant sigh came from behind as Ace grumbled and put away his claymore. "What are you doing here, Zee?" he huffed.

"You know, Aceius, that hurts!" Zeendria's hands flew dramatically to her heart. "After all this time, I thought we were more than family, that we had bonded, that we were friends." Her eyes gleamed and the theatrics had Ro grinning. "You finally bring Ro home… Is it okay that I call you Ro?" she asked, not waiting for a response before carrying on. "You bring her here to our lovely realm and you choose not to include me? My heart is shattered, Ace, abs-o-lutely devastated."

Ro could barely contain her amusement as the sly girl linked arms with her and led her around the fire.

"Although, I know that if it were anyone other than me, they wouldn't still be standing, so I guess I owe you my thanks. Anyway, Sparrow, it is a pleasure to meet you after all this time! You, my dear friend, are the talk of the town, and what a lovely topic to discuss, by the way." Zeendria winked as Ro found herself being pulled down to a sit beside her.

She was thrown off, but not in a bad way. "Well, Zeendria, it's nice to meet you as well."

"Move over," Ace muttered, exasperated as he plopped himself between them, a grimace on his face. "You know full well why I couldn't tell you she was here. And keep up the flirting, Zee," he added. "I'll make sure to let Adyra know. She won't like you very much come Christmas."

This information exploded a light bolt of joy in Ro's brain. "Wait..." She leaned across Ace. "You know Adyra?"

Zeendria chucked, pushing down her own hood. "Of course, I know her; in fact, you could say we have a... unique friendship." She winked before pulling what looked like sandwiches out of her small bag and handing one to Ace. "I thought you might be hungry, what with running away from the house. Your poor mother is absolutely devastated, not to mention your father's raging disappointment."

Ace's look shot daggers but he accepted the sandwich. "Yeah, well, my mother shouldn't have lied, and Dad could use a lesson in disappointment."

He was exhausted, Ro realized, bringing her hand

to his shoulder in comfort. Zee offered her a sandwich.

"Thank you." Ro shot her a grin. "I was feeling a bit peckish. You don't mind me asking though, why did you just hide out in the trees? If you're not with them, then you could have joined us." She took a bite, her stomach dancing at the taste of the delicious bread.

"When I first started following you, it was out of curiosity. I overheard Acey here yelling with his father then running to get you. Honestly, I just got lucky that he cast the cloaking charm where I was hiding. If he hadn't, I would've lost you for sure. I could also tell something was going on with you two and I would nev-er" —she sent a racy smile— "want to interrupt that."

Heat rushed to Ro's face as she watched Ace smirk into his food.

"Nothing was going on between us," she insisted. "We were just having a discussion, that's all."

"Sureee," Zeendria said with a playful tilt of her chin. "Anyway, I wasn't going make an appearance, but then I could tell that Ace here…" she nudged her cousin "…was going to tell you the tale of the lost family. Out of all the tales our history professor used to recite at the Halls of Ivy, this one was my absolute favourite!" Her squeal of excitement caused Ro to jump as she swal-lowed the last of her food. Ace leaned away from the noise.

"The tale of the lost family?" Ro repeated slowly. "But I was asking about my connection to the Nefarie not another tale."

"I know." Zeendria rolled her eyes. "This tale

though might give you the answers you're looking for." She slapped Ace's shoulder. "Come on, we both know that's where you were heading. Give the girl her answers!"

Sighing, he cracked his neck. "Hmm, Interdictum, better known as the lost family." Ace looked to the sky. "I'll begin where we left off then."

As he spoke, Ro found herself leaning into his words, hopeful to leave this conversation with a better understanding; convinced this was how she would find her own family.

"King Breenus stayed alive just long enough for the birth of his son, Arturo. After he passed, Arturo was practically raised by the kingdom itself. He was a smart boy, growing to be an even wiser man. Strong and stubborn with a powerful magic, he was destined to become a great leader, one who stood for equal representation of all. After the Halls of Ivy, he applied under his Mother's approval, to take an apprenticeship training with the Fae diplomats stationed at the high court of Skyen Kingdom."

"The Elven Kingdom?" Ro remembered.

"Yes, a beautiful place made of stone and marble," Zeendria chimed in, her face beaming with excitement. "Beautiful with rising formations of the land and forever connected with the earth. Elves are normally more proficient with magics dependent on earth and fire. They crafted their home to be around the source."

"Anyway," Ace said, shooting them both a pointed look. "When his apprenticeship was approved, Arturo packed up his things, refused the tradition of a small gathering of guards, and chose only to take his lifelong best friend: a meek man from a good family, high in Fae court. This man was always fighting to get ahead and would use whatever techniques he could to rise to the top, but Arturo trusted him as they had a bond most thought to be closer than brothers, and together they embarked to Skyen. The thing to remember about this friend was that his strong sense of loyalty would shift depending on what benefited him the most.

"The journey was short, and they soon arrived, greeted wholeheartedly by the Elves and the few Fae who had decided to live in the kingdom."

"Do Fae and Elves not normally live together?" Ro asked.

"In the small towns and villages throughout they do," Ace answered. "But normally, those living in the kingdoms keep to themselves. This has a lot to do with the type of magic both are prone to and the location of both kingdoms. Although this has been changing throughout the years."

"Come on, Fabler," Zeendria cut in. "Keep the story moving."

"Okay, okay," he said, waving her off. "After the two had met with the high court and rested in their rooms, they were honoured with a ball."

"One the likes of which no one had seen in ages!" Zeendria interrupted wistfully.

"I thought you wanted me to tell the story."

"Get on with it, then." She gestured playfully.

Ro chuckled at their antics. They were like bickering children, happy to have a reason to laugh.

Ace cleared his throat. "As I was saying…" He shot a pointed look at Zeendria. "They were escorted to the ball alongside other diplomats, and introduced as royalty. Arturo protested this, hating the prim and proper rules of society he would have to follow. He only wanted to strengthen the bonds between Elves and Fae, hoping that one day they could all live together without any discrepancy. Then, as it often happens in these types of stories, he met her."

"Her?" Ro echoed, already invested in yet another mystical tale, although she couldn't see how this was going to provide any answers.

"Yes." Zeendria's tone had dropped to a wistful chime. "Her. The daughter of the high court's leader, destined to be ruler to all things Elven. Just as Arturo was to all things Fae. Dressed in a gown laden with blue, she spun around the groups of people, freely talking and mesmerizing all. Her name was Rinna and she too detested this ball she was forced to attend, but the second she met him, well, the sight-givers call it fate, and boy did she fall hard!"

"Zeendria!" Ace groaned. "Do you want me to tell it or not?"

"Okay, okay, fine," she said dramatically, throwing her hands up as Ace continued.

"Over the first few months that he was there, Rinna and Arturo spent every second possible together. When he wasn't with her, Arturo spent his time learning all he could to strengthen magical relations, trying to win the Elvin leaders favour. Though they were forbidden to be together, their closest friends helped them escape for little moments at a time, dates if you could call them that, where they could be themselves and be alone."

Something about this struck a nerve with Ro and she cocked her head in confusion. "Why couldn't they be together? I mean, why exactly was it forbidden? That's a really harsh word."

Ace cleared his throat again as Zeendria grew quiet.

"The bonds between Elves and Fae have always been good, for the most part. Both leaders tend to work together, and since coming to this world there has always been an elected Fae king and queen by both sides of magical blood. Yet um… personal relationships between Fae and Elves have not always been seen in the best light. In fact, until recent years, they have been looked down upon, those couples being seen as a disgrace."

"That's ridiculous!" Ro exclaimed.

"I agree," he answered calmly. "But times are changing, and in non-royal-related families it is becoming more normal and accepted. But back then, it was not."

"And now that has changed?" Ro found herself pitching in again.

"Yes and no. It is more accepted, but those of mixed Fae and Elven blood still have to fight more than they should to find their place in this world." His eyes darted worriedly toward Zeendria when it suddenly dawned on her.

"Wait so…?"

"Yeah," Zeendria interrupted. "My mother is Fae, Ace's aunt. But my father. Well…" She pushed back her hair to reveal slightly pointed ears. "He's Elvin. It's why my skin is purple, and I have these ears. Elven genetics tend to bounce off the magic in your blood, changing your aspects a bit." She looked down.

"Honestly, I think that's really cool," Ro said quickly. "I'd love blue skin, but I can't even tan."

"Be careful what you wish for, good looking." Zeendria winked. "It might be closer to coming true than you know. But thank you."

"Zee here has the ability to cast a charm to look more human if she wishes," Ace said. "But I think it's good that she doesn't use it."

"That's really cool," Ro said. "Why would a charm like that be needed anyway?"

"For travelling to the mortal realm." Zeendria smirked. "Normally, travel is forbidden, but there are special cases where it's permitted, and I wouldn't want to go scaring away all those pesky humans with my charming looks now would I? Any Fae or Elf that travels through the realms has to have a glamour cast to look like a mortal."

This made sense. Ro could only imagine the reactions an Elf would get at a shopping mall. "Anyway," Zeendria said. "Back to my favourite story from my favourite cousin."

Ace grinned at them. "Right, so toward the end of Arturo's trip, they were spending almost every night together when Rinna understood that something had changed. While her lover was in an evaluation meeting with the high courts, she had sought the help of her friend who was training to be a healer. Together they had realized the impossible had happened. Rinna rushed to Arturo and told him the moment they had a chance together… she was pregnant. She was scared he would be upset, but she was surprised by his happiness. Right there, in front of both their friends and unborn baby, he decided to turn away from what would be expected; he declared he would never leave her.

"They had a choice to make and went to her father right away. You see, Arturo had thought that he had earned enough favour for them to be accepted as a couple, but he was wrong. The leader of the Elven high court was furious and devastated. While he supported relationships between all of magical blood, he knew that the people would never accept this between those of royal blood, let alone the future leaders of both kingdoms. He refused to accept them being together and insisted that Arturo leave and Rinna not have the child."

"Wait," Ro said. "I still don't understand. If the people were accepting of it between themselves, why would they have an issue with a royal couple of both magical bloods bringing a baby into the world together?"

"Because," Zeendria sighed, "a long time ago, there was an old bat of a woman, an oracle you could call her, who made a prediction that a royal child born of both bloods could bring nothing but the end of life as all knew it to be. The child would teeter the line of good and evil, bringing chaos to the land."

"Ridiculous," Ro protested.

"That's what the young couple thought," Ace said, smiling. "So in the dead of night, they snuck out to be married by their friends, creating a bond that could not be undone. Then on horseback, they left Skyen Kingdom. It was the last time Rinna would ever see her home or her family. They arrived at the kingdom of Merwin the next morning and pleaded to Arturo's mother, the ruling Queen Elsina, for assistance. While she believed in them and thought the oracle's tale was rubbish, she also knew that as long as they stayed, the unborn child would never be safe. Sources had told her that word of the couple began to spread and the Nefarie were overjoyed. They somehow had gotten it into their heads that this child could be turned to their side. That this child's magic, which had the potential to contain unprecedented power due to both parents' genetics, would be the tool they needed to succeed in their goals. You see, most would already fear this unborn baby because, for the first time ever, there would be a true ruler of both kingdoms, and there was nothing the houses or common people could do about it. This would be a child of mixed blood and both Fae and Elven abilities with magic unlike anyone had ever seen."

"So, what happened?" Ro whispered against the biting wind.

"Elsina decided the best way to bring happiness to

all was if the child was raised in a world without magic. In the dark of the next early morning, she said goodbye to her son and new daughter-in-law with a torn and heavy heart, as she knew that she could never see them again. They were granted permission to leave this realm for the mortal realm. Bound by a blood promise to hide among humans and to never, of free will, return for the safety of their child, who would be raised unknowing of who they really were. Both parents giving up their royal rights. Yet she knew that while she could never have communication with them again, she could make sure they were protected, and so she set up a task force of a few people she trusted around them. Their two friends, the spoiled son of a high Fae lord and the Elvin healer, were to live with them as permanent protection, as well as have visitations from a highly trusted Fae family to make sure that the protection charms around them were kept up and well."

Ro's heart ached. "So, after all that they had to leave their home? Just because they were in love and wanted to raise their child together?"

"Well," Ace continued slowly. "They were erased from the documentation of official royal lines, neither court nor kingdom spoke of them again."

"The Elvish high leader took it pretty hard, but since there was no official proof of anything, he couldn't retaliate," Zeendria added, eyes darting to Ace's before he carried on.

"Unless it was used as an example in an advanced history lesson, it was something no one was permitted to speak of. That's why they are called the lost family, because it's fresh enough in people's minds to know it happened, yet momentous enough for the history books."

"And no one ever heard of this family again? What about the child?" Ro asked.

"Well she…" Ace began.

"Is you!" Zeendria interrupted with glee. "Don't you get it, Ro? The child of both Fae and Elven blood; the one powerful enough to either unite or destroy us all; why you're here and were shielded from all of this. And now, finally, you're home!"

CHAPTER TWELVE

Numb. Her body was numb; every cell stiff and cold. *MOVE, GET UP, DO SOMETHING!* her muffled mind screamed, as she felt the damp ground seeping through her clothes and into her bones.

Every interaction with her friends and family whirled around her memory, stuck in a jarring loop.

She was searching, prying, begging for a sign, some sort of gesture or flag that should have stood out to her. Her mom was always a little too quiet and her dad booming loud, yet they had never hinted this way. Even when she moved in with Althea, life proceeded normal-ish, considering the circumstances. Between classes online and dinner conversations, nothing seemed out of the ordinary. Sure, she caught a strange look clouding the impish woman's features on the odd occasion, but that could have been boiled down to worry. Ro squinted against the fire, her head throbbing. Wouldn't she have noticed something? But nothing changed. Other than those days disappearing… "Ugh," she moaned as the throbbing increased. She tried to reflect on that day, the one she had lost. It felt like if she could just remember that moment… then maybe something would make sense, but the harder she tried to focus, the more her vision blurred.

"Whoa, hey, look at me. Deep breaths." Two bold eyes met hers. "Five seconds in, five seconds out. Time between the worlds can get a little hazy, combine that with whatever they did to your head and well… just focus on the facts we have."

"I… What?" Ro sputtered. She wanted to protest, but too many details slid into the correct slots. For one, Ace's family came to see her once a year, just like the family that was granted visitation from the tale. They were friends with her parents and lived in this other world. Two: Ace was right, as much as she hated to admit it. Her parents had never told her anything about their upbringing or any other family; it was silly that she had never thought to ask. And three: the two friends who left the world as well matched up perfectly with Althea's skills in medicine and Peri's higher-than-thou mindset.

"Hmmph," she smouldered, rolling her eyes to these thoughts. Who was she kidding? Ro couldn't deny she had seen magic. She had travelled through a freaking tree, for crying out loud. Yet, there was no way she could just accept this, right? It was just her luck that time took this particular moment to catch up.

"Hugs help panic attacks, right?" Zeendria said, wrapping two surprisingly toned arms around Ro. "You know, because of the pressure and—"

Ro pried herself away gently as she tried to collect her dazed thoughts. Even though the facts fit, Ro knew she needed more proof, she just couldn't understand this. She decided it was crazy. The other girl had clearly been misinformed, or had gotten some bad information somewhere down the line, that was it... She needed hard, undeniable proof. "Ace?" His name slid out of her mouth. "Please tell your sweet, disillusioned cousin here that she's wrong. There's no way I'm some child of a lost family."

Zeendria's smile slowly dropped and Ro turned away from her, the pit in her stomach growing as she waited for his confirmation. The air around them grew cold and tense. Her thunderous heart pounded in her ears. *Either give me the evidence, or admit that you're were wrong. Why wasn't he saying anything at all?* If there ever was a time to swoop in with annoying tidbits of factual information, now would be it! Yet, as the silence continued, she could feel his calculated gaze shift between the two of them. Something about the way he didn't leap to her reassurance concerned her, something was off yet again.

Twisting slowly to focus her attention to the left, she saw Ace was sitting still enough to be a statue, except for the slow and careful movement of his eyes.

"Aceius?" Her voice came out firm and slow. "Tell her it's not true."

His breath was a long, slow hiss. "Oh, she shouldn't have said that… why couldn't she just keep it zipped?! Just until Merwin. We could have explained everything in Merwin." He blew out an exasperated sigh to the moon above. "I'm afraid, that while it came out a bit brash, she speaks the truth. I wanted to tell you sooner, we all did, but Elsina forbade it. You're not supposed to know. Granted, this whole thing was supposed to be a lot smoother too, but still."

Ro flinched back from his words. "No!"

"Yes!" Zeendria piped up again, much more serious this time. "Sparrow, you are the child of the lost family. The oracle was talking about you. If we get you the proper lessons, you'll—"

"No." It seemed like that was the only word her stuttering brain could form. Two sides of her fought against each other, raging war. *It's true, you know it is, you've always known,* one side screamed. *"They have the wrong girl, if you don't make them see that then you'll just be setting yourself up for another disappointment,"* the other side taunted.

Ace sighed again. "Ro, it's you. Why do you think I brought you here?"

That's when she felt it. Something in her snapped.

In a blind haste, she jumped up to face them both. "Zeendria, Zee, dear…" Ro focused her attention on her solemn companion. "There is no way, and I mean none at all, that is me. I'm sorry to get your hopes up. Because, darling, I think I would know if I were some lost magical being."

"Except you wouldn't!" Zee insisted, looking to Ace for help, but Ro wasn't quite done.

She was going to have to break this down for them. "So apparently everyone here lost a few brain cells on the trip through this wonderlandesque adventure. Okay, fine, let's do this, Zeendria. Let me officially introduce myself since both of you seem to have dropped a few marbles on the way here." She looked between them wildly before gesturing to herself. "I," she emphasized, "am Sparrow. Ro for short. But you already know that. Nice to make your acquaintance! I am a normal, plain as the day is long, HUMAN girl from a small town out in the boondocks, a town so far up nowhere lane you get lost trying to find it." Her voice seemed to increase with every word. "While I would LOVE to help you out and be this person you two think I am, I simply am NOT! Now, if we could possibly go back to the point before you two were disillusioned, that would be greatly appreciated."

Zeendria's sad chuckle drifted on the wind. "You really don't get it do you, Ro?"

"Get what?"

"Ro…" Ace cautiously started.

Her head snapped toward him. "What?"

"Why do you think you are here?" he asked. "Mortals are forbidden to know of Magica. Breaking that rule is punishable with a fate far beyond that of death."

"Oh, I don't know, maybe I am here because I have been chased down and all but tormented by some crazy group that calls themselves the Nefarie!" Why was no one understanding her?

His sigh was so heavy she could feel it through her mounting hysteria.

"I asked you to really think about what was happening around you. Why do you think the Nefarie are after you?"

Ro turned so her back was warmed against the heat of the fire. "Okay. You want me to think? Then let me just bounce some things off the two of you here." She found herself so caught up in her own dramatics she almost missed the pained look they shared. "You expect me to believe that my mom was, sorry is, what? Some kind of Elf? A thing that I only relate to as tinkering around the North Pole, by the way."

"Hey, rude!" Zeendria gasped.

Every cell in Ro's body told her to fight this, to get through to the real answers. "On top of that insanity, you're telling me that my dad, that overtly loud man, is some sort of flying fairy prince?" She looked at the both of them incredulously. Surely, they had to see how ridiculous this was.

"Fae, but yes." Ace corrected.

"Fae, Elf, I don't care." She focused on the two of them. "The point is that *you* believe, and you want *me* to believe, that the normal, *human* parents I have seen almost every day of my entire life, are magical fairy tale creatures, and I am some combination of the two."

Their slow nods dumbfounded her.

"One problem guys..." She gestured up and down her body. "In case you haven't noticed, I don't exactly look like anything other than human."

Ace cautiously chimed in. "Any Fae or Elf that crossed the border from Magica must conceal any non-human identifiers. So, your parents would have always masked theirs, and from birth, your true features, any inhuman ones you might have that is, would have been concealed as well."

Stricken, Ro paused. "So you're telling me that I could look like a completely different person?" she asked, dumbfounded as visions of Morgan La Fey and Medusa danced in her head.

"No, no. Ace, you're scaring her!" Zeendria smacked his arm. "You might just have some Fae or Elvin features you don't know of yet."

"Yet? What? Should I expect to randomly grow wings or something?"

"Fae don't really have wings, remember? That's a myth, magic uses air for flight. Anyway, you are not going to randomly change or grow a new appendage."

Ro stopped double checking herself for any weird abnormality.

Ace shrugged as if it was no big deal. "You just might one day notice your ears are pointer, small things like that."

"Yeah, not knowing for sure what I look like, check one on my list of things that aren't a problem!" She deflated to the ground. "Okay..." Ro barely recognized her drained tone. "Are we absolutely sure this isn't a case of mistaken identity? You're telling me that my parents were of two different magical races who were never supposed to be, or were even allowed to be, together?"

"Yes and no," Ace said.

Both he and Zeendria leaned forward cautiously, as if afraid she would combust. "Marriage between Fae and Elves is not illegal or looked down upon in these days, the issue is that the higher houses and royal families have never mixed blood before by giving birth to a child of both magics, having the strongest magics of both would mean unspeakable power. You are something like we have never seen, and the unknown scares people, even if it's just a baby."

"Oh, and I suppose this is where you tell me that all the weird freaky happenings in my life are because of my magic and that just solves everything right?" It was official, in that moment she hated Zeendria's sarcastic grin. "One problem guys. I wasn't kidding when I said my life is normal. I have never had the slightest weird occurrence that can point to magic, at least not the kind of magic I've seen." Peri's stone-cold face as he casually willed the book across the room crept into her mind, giving her a chill.

"You wouldn't," Ace murmured.

"What?"

"You wouldn't have seen any magic. Not only is it forbidden in the realm of mortals, this isn't some fantasy movie, magic doesn't just happen."

"He's right," Zeendria agreed. "It's genetic, connected to what we call a life-force. Others might call it a soul. Magic needs to be trained up, practiced for the user to even be able to do simple charms let alone massive spells. If you didn't know you had the ability to use magic or how to use it, then there is a really good chance you would have lived your whole life thinking you are as normal as any human passing you on the street."

Ro's head hurt. Her insides screamed that they were right, that she needed to search deeper. Almost like there was a block in her brain she just couldn't get past. "But…" she hesitantly spoke. "If that were true, if all of this were true, then wouldn't my parents have said *something*? There is no way they could have let me go my whole life in the dark!"

Her companions had settled into their spots, like they knew this wasn't going to be accepted without a struggle. The tired lines from earlier smoothed into a shared understanding and patience.

"They were bound by a Sponsum, a truth curse. If they ever let anything slip, or breathed one slight mention of this to you—or anyone else for that matter—a curse would be set upon the blood of your family, including that of Elsina, slowly torturing each of you to unknown ends. Only a few have ever survived a broken Sponsum, they are but former shells of themselves, in a state of such constant pain they're better off dead."

A shudder ran through her at the thought of this broken curse. If she was truly this lost person or whatever, then that didn't bode well for her parents. Determination flowed through her, eyes blazing as she looked up once more. "Show me."

They both looked alarmed; one unsure, the other grinning wildly.

"We really shouldn't…" Ace said.

"Yes, we should."

"No, Zee, she's not ready."

"Yes, she is."

"Listen, if we teach her improper—"

"Oh, screw your orders and—"

"It's not about orders. I'm trying to keep both of you safe."

"Safe!? Ha! You didn't even know I was here! I'm—"

"Enough!" Ro said. She refused to take the backseat in her life any longer. "Ace, grow up, you're supposed to be my friend, and yet you have possibly allowed me to live my entire life without knowing any of this," her arms swung wide. "Without knowing who I truly am? Just because of some orders? I need… no, I deserve and want to see magic up close and personal without the threat of it hurting me or anyone else. If the Nefarie are truly after me, then my best shot, my family's best shot, is to understand." The cloak drifted off her as she sat straight and focused.

"I'm not keeping things from you because I want to, Ro, we all just want to keep you safe." He ran an anxious hand through his hair. "You weren't there when Adyra and I got the call that you had been attacked and your parents were missing. I just, we just, couldn't lose you like that. It has always been my family's duty to protect yours, even if my parents have forgotten that promise, I haven't." Pain stabbed his tired features.

"Aceius…" Determination shook her tone. "I am stronger than you think, and I don't need your protection, but thank you. I'm not asking you to fight for me, and obviously I'm not asking your parents either. Whatever happened that night, I don't blame you."

Zee's arm went to his as he shook his head toward the ground. "For the record, I have never, ever thought it was right to keep this from you. That's why I have always been so bad at taking orders, but that night..." He paused, collecting his thoughts. "That night, we thought we lost you, and I can't help but think that if I had listened more at school, or paid more attention to my orders, then you would have been safe and your parents would be here with us, telling you this themselves, or well, probably not, but, I'm just trying to protect you now more than we did then."

Guilt edged into her gut as she watched them. Zeendria offered Ace some sad reassurance, arm resting on her cousin's, whose ridged face blazed with determination. Ro hadn't even thought to consider their perspectives... In the beginning she had been so scared, so lost, that she hadn't cared to listen to her friend's truths. Even now that she had seen this place and the possibility of what it could do, she had never once stopped to consider how this was affecting anyone else but her. For the first time, Ro found herself giving them a thorough look over. Of course, she hadn't missed the purplish circles under Ace's eyes. She had just ignored them to focus on her own problems. Adyra, on the other hand, had seemed okay, but maybe she was just a bit too happy, too alright. Perhaps Adyra had been forcing the cheerfulness for everyone else, maybe she had been worried too and Ro was too wrapped up in herself to know. Zeendria, Ro didn't know at all. She could be fine, but there was so much Ro didn't know about her that she couldn't really tell.

Ro's cheeks burned a cherry red, rivalling her wild locks, she was ashamed not to have noticed she was not the only one struggling. She had been so angry at their secrets, but she had a few of herself, didn't she? Like the dreams… something about them was too real. There was so much she hadn't told her friends, and she had ignored their concern for her own. *No more of that,* she decided. No longer would she act without thinking for others, especially those she had to rely on. *From this point,* Ro told herself, *I will give into the adventure.*

"I'm sorry, Ace, that you ever felt like you had to take any blame. None of this was yours or Adyra's fault."

He looked up in protest.

"That's neither here nor there, I just don't want you to carry it with you any further. Apparently…" a deep sigh left her, like a weight floating from her shoulders, "there's a lot I need to learn about myself, and about my parents. When we see Adyra again, I'm going to speak to her as well, because there are some things I haven't been completely honest with you about either." Remembering the Nefarie made her shudder. "I want to sit down, to tell you everything, and I want to listen, to learn more. Not just some tale, but everything from your perspectives. I feel like the more information I have, the better."

His eyebrows shot up. "What haven't you told us?"

"I'll tell you. But before I do, I'm asking that you no longer look at it as protecting me. Everything I know has changed, and I'm just here trying to fit all the pieces together again. I need a friend, not a bodyguard."

Zeendria's thinned lips darted into a mischievous grin as she spoke again. "I think that can be arranged. Don't think you're getting away with your secrets though."

"Like you don't have some of your own still." Ace's laugh was lighter this time. "I guess then, if you're up for a later night, Zee could show you a few things."

Zeendria all but squealed with glee, breaking her cool girl demeanour. "Sit down, sit down." Nimble palms danced in front of the flames.

Ro's body hummed with anticipation. Sure, she had experienced some magic over the last few days, but this was a chance to understand it, and possibly learn it herself. The cold brisk air burned her unblinking eyes as she watched the younger girl glide in front of her. It was like a form of art. Hands danced together, clasping before forming a triangle, chasing each other around an invisible ball as their owner looked on with ease. The air crackled, exposing tiny droplets of water. They pulled together out of thin air. Finally, the swaying slowed, one palm circling the droplets, the other grazing their tops and steadily thrusting forwards, a solid flat palm stopping before the flickering flames.

"*CHROUS VENTI.*"

The air sizzled with electricity. Powerful gusts shoved

past them, whipping the loose ends of her locks. Ro sat back, stunned. One moment she had been mesmerized by the slow movements of water in the air, and the next… her thoughts trailed off as she shook herself out of her stupor. The vibrant flickering flames had stilled in place. No longer was there a controlled leaping of chaotic heat; instead, ice glistened in the starlight. Not only was it frozen, but to her amazement, the iced flames twisted and glided, meeting at the top to form a delicate oak tree.

"What… how?"

Zeendria giggled and shrugged. "Simple really." She sat close once more. "My mom is really good at fire and air magic. I'm not so sure what my dad is prone to, but it must have something to do with water because I draw from the air and water sources to aid my spells. That was a simple charm I picked up a couple of years ago. I just drew the moisture around us and froze it, using a breeze to construct it around the fire."

"That was…" Ro's mind was blown. "That was amazing, Zeendria, really."

The other girl grinned. "It's Zee. Zeendria's just too stiff a name for friends. And dear, you haven't seen nothin' yet."

It had only been a few days, yet Ro could no longer imagine a world without magic. "So you can only use air and water to help you because that's what your parents were good at?"

"Yeah, it's all about your genetics." She rotated her hand, turning her palm upwards. A small tornado hopped in the centre to the beat of her tone. "I'm lucky though because I feel really connected to my assisting elements. Those who don't can struggle to find their place with spells." With the drop of her hand the spiralling storm was gone again.

"What about you?" Ro grinned toward their silent friend, eager to see what elements he used to assist his magic.

Ace cleared his throat. "Mine's not nearly as flashy, most Fae rely on both air and fire to assist in magics, just like most Elves use water and land. That's why the cities or kingdoms of both are heavily influenced by them. Zee here is special though." He gestured to the smirking girl. "Because she has an Elven father and a Fae mother, both bloodlines duked it out to give her the ability to control air and water. I, on the other hand, follow more closely to my Fae ancestry." He flexed his fingers with a whispered, "*Atramentum.*" The air shimmered and Ro leaned forward for a closer look. His left hand curled, almost pointed toward her as his finger curved, gliding through the air. Sparking letters burned into the empty space: "Hello Sparrow." She could feel the heat emanating from it as he drew a line underneath, a mini fire hovering above the land.

"So, you rely on fire? Or fire and air?" Her enthusiasm bubbled out. "You used a, what was that? A spell or a charm? Zee didn't say anything when she created the tornado."

Her companions laughed.

"I rely on both, but my air magic is weaker," Ace explained. "I trained up my abilities to use fire at the Halls of Ivy. And no, you don't always need to use a spell—that was a spell, by the way. I know you've probably figured this out, but these abilities come with a cost. The more you use, the more energy is taken from you."

"Energy?" It was hard to put a picture to such an indescribable thing. "If you've never done magic before, small spells might wear you out, make you tired. That's why we go to school here to practice. Eventually, you build up a tolerance so that things like this don't wear you out." He waved his wrist though the letters. One by one they puffed into smoke and out of existence.

"Like Breenus and Elsina? Being drained from such a powerful spell?"

"Exactly," Ace said. "Draining too much has physical effects on the body. It can age you… or worse."

Shivers shot down her spine.

"Uggghhhhh!" Zee interrupted, slouching against them. "Don't just tell her all the negatives. Ro, magic is unbelievably cool. There's this connection to the elements that support you, like nothing you can ever replace. It's like they are living and breathing through you. Besides, you'll have us here to help you train, so you don't have to worry about using too much. We won't let you."

"Wait…" Ro gapped at the other girl. "I can train with magic…? I don't even know how to use any elements."

Zee's eyes sparked with joy. "Oh, darling, don't worry, we'll figure out your elements. Maybe tonight even."

"Tonight?"

"Whoa…" Aces tone slid through their conversation like a hot knife through butter, cutting though her excitement as well. "You still have your stuff to share remember? Something you've been hiding from us?"

Ro groaned. The dreams. She knew she had to tell them about the stupid dreams. It wasn't that she didn't want to. It just wasn't her favourite thing to speak about. Both of them felt too real, almost as if she left her sleeping body somewhere while also physically being somewhere else completely. Groaning, she shifted toward them again.

If she just said she wasn't ready to talk about it, they would respect that, Ro was positive. It would be easier that way too, but something in her said no, and screamed for her to tell them. Deep in her gut, Ro knew letting the truth out there would make her feel better. It was now or never. Better late to the party than to never show up, right? With a short sigh, she began her tale.

"It started with a dream."

CHAPTER THIRTEEN

Visions of cloaked, mysterious Nefarie members danced in the simmering smoke, sending chills up all of their spines. Her friends stared at her, baffled. For the first time since she landed amongst the swirling leaves, Zee sat utterly still, her face parallelized in a state of shock. Their silence settled in the coals at her feet.

"How long?" Ace's voice echoed through the night. "How long have you had these dreams?"

"Just the once or twice. Honestly, I never dreamed much before the accident—or if I did, I could never recall them."

"You said you had nightmares? Of falling?"

"Well, yeah," she affirmed. "Almost every night since moving in with Althea. It was the same dream over and over. I'd be shoved into this never-ending hole, not necessarily falling, but trapped. I knew I had to save myself, but there was nothing I could do. That's when the screams would start. My parent's voices, yours, Althea's, Adyra's… I always woke to Althea's voice." The memory of the thin older woman waking her with lavender tea comforted her darkened thoughts.

Zee groaned, lowering her body into a horizontal position on the ground. "It sounds like a bunch of hogwash to me. You went through a traumatic event, one that your brain can recall, but you can't. It's no wonder you were having nightmares. Nothing to worry about, beautiful."

Ro couldn't tell if the girl's sleepy wink was flirtation or exhaustion.

Collecting his thoughts with the calculated patience of an old sea turtle building its nest, Ace sighed. "What if your subconscious was trying to tell you something though… a piece of the time that was stolen from you? In your other dream," he continued. "Were they by a river? At night?"

Her nod was slow and cautious. She hadn't told them that much, only of the two figures she had seen.

"And you said they talked of a mole? Someone named Olrod?" A chill that had nothing to do with the wind accompanied his words.

"What's with the twenty questions, Sherlock?" Zee knocked his shoulder.

"Brambiee Coast." His voice was so low Ro only knew it meant something by Zee's sudden stare.

"You don't think…?" The girl left her question unfinished.

"I don't know… honestly. It seems like a possibility though."

"It can't be. That gift died out long ago."

"I know…" He groaned. It was like they had forgotten she could still hear them.

"So. Just ignore it. One fluke. No biggie."

"The dream she's talking about? It actually happened. Adyra was there, Zee. After she left Aylee she was assigned to the west side of Brambiee Coast, tracking a lead given by Olrod Contos." Zee's face fell. "A sightseer."

"A sightseer?" she chimed in. "As in someone who sees things or…?"

"Welcome to history 101, Sparrow darling. It seems you're learning all about our ancient pasts and traditions tonight." The other girl smiled invitingly, gesturing as if welcoming a crowd of invisible spectators.

"Back when this land was new there used to be people, a special force you could say, who could predict things by, well, this is going to sound crazy…" Ace said while rolling his eyes.

Ro snorted. "You just told me magic was real, I have it, and oh, I might wake up one day looking like an Elf. I can handle crazy."

His pointed look caused her to laugh.

"Their genetic ties to magic were strong enough it allowed them to walk through a dreamscape, picking up occurrences from the future. If they were lucky enough, they could have a clear moment in another plain while their physical body remained asleep."

It wasn't the weirdest thing she had seen or heard on this trip, why not add dreams of walking future-knowers to the mix? "And you think… you think I am one of them? Or I—"

"No," Zee sat up hurriedly. "No way you are a dream-walker. I mean, sure your magic has the potential to be strong and powerful, but dream-walkers?!" She scoffed. "They died off a long time ago."

"Died off?"

"No… not… well…" Zee sighed again. "Sorry, I'm tired, and this is all a little outlandish for me. Um. How should I put it? Dream-walkers were people of our past that we learned of in school They were our versions of fairy tales. We also learned that over time their skillset was no longer needed, seeing as we are safe in this land without the threat of mortals and war. There was no reason to need the security of dream-walkers, so as we evolved that power was unfortunately left behind, lost and unable to be retrieved again. Our bodies recognized there wasn't a need for it anymore."

"So, they don't exist, these dream-walkers?"

"Not anymore."

"Well, a version of them does," Ace interjected, his voice sliding though the conversation. "Those alive today have a talent for a short burst of visions. We call them sight-givers though. They can only see a limited possibility of someone's close future. A very flexible future that can change at any given time. They don't have anywhere near the powers of a dream-walker though."

"So, what does that mean for me?" Ro wondered.

He sighed. "Honestly, I think that means we should speak to a mentor when we reach the City of Merwin. They should be able to give us more information. I don't want to tell you anything that's wrong, especially given everything you've been through."

Not knowing sucked, but Ro found herself grateful that she was now being given the truth. It made her feel one step closer to finding her parents. The tense silence embraced them once more and she sunk into retrospection. It had been a long night and an even longer past few weeks. She was no longer sad, alone, or even scared. If the Nefarie wanted her, then they would have to wait until she at least found her family again. Nothing was more important than that, and for the first time since moving to Claudaith she felt like she had control over her life again; she had choices. Also, she would never admit this to them, but it was nice to have people she could trust and connect to in her life once more. Ro hadn't realized just how much she missed normal everyday relationships. The crazy thing was, through all the chaos and drama everything finally felt alright. Like she was where she was meant to be.

"I know!" Zee leapt to her feet, abounding with joy once more. "Wanna try and see what elements you are drawn to?" Moonlight danced off her mischievous grin.

Timid excitement rattled Ro. She hadn't even thought about using magic herself. "Sure, I mean, how would we do that?"

"Come on." Ace pulled her to her feet. "We'll show you some basic charms in each form. The one—"

"—or ones," Zee interrupted, laughing.

"Okay. Tell me what to do!"

The cousins shared a cautious look, but Ro didn't care. For the first time in days, she felt excited and free.

"Your mind needs to be clear and focused. Take a deep breath and follow me." Ace moved so they formed a small circle. He inhaled deeply and raised his hands. As he exhaled long and slow, he pushed his flattened palm downwards.

Ro's hands shook as she tried to match his practiced and steady pace, rounding in circles and joining both her hands together in a calming dance. Something about it reminded her of the meditations her old therapist had suggested long ago. If only she could see her now—standing in the middle of the night, shrouded by trees, and swaying her hands in gentle, trancelike movements.

Ace's voice surrounded her. "Close your eyes and continue to repeat the triangle.

Her eyelids sank until all she saw was dark.

"Good, Ro. Now take some deep breaths for me. In through the nose for four, hold for four, and out for six, okay?"

She tried her best not to lose focus and keep up the movements, feeling a bit like a fish out of water as she heard the chant continue.

"And two three four, hold two three four, out two three four five six. Again, two three four, hold two three, four, out two three four five six."

This continued until she almost forgot that she was supposed to be counting.

"Now, Ro, breathe normal. Picture a space as black as the night sky. An empty canvas. Picture a gold fire in the shape of your movements. A small lit triangle sparking to life with each move."

Stuck in a trance, the triangle came to life behind her eyelids, as every other sensation fell away.

"Now, picture the elements. Each one having their own safe and cozy space inside that triangle. Earth at the tippy top, water in the far left corner, fire all the way to the bottom right, spirit in the middle. Connecting them all together."

She held the image in her mind.

"Can you see them?"

She nodded and whispered, "I can feel the heat from the fire I am imagining."

Sparks of shock flew through her arm, causing her to stumble slightly. She continued the motions though.

"Good, Sparrow. That's good. Spend a moment feeling them, let them get to know you, and then on my count, push your hand through the triangle, dragging the ones that call to you outside of the triangle walls."

Which ones was she supposed to call out of the triangle? What if none of them responded?

"It's okay if you don't know which ones," he said as if he could sense her questions. "Just call to them and they will listen to your heart. Now, on my count, one…"

Okay imaginary elements; it's now or never.

"Two…"

Please come to me… please.

"Three…"

No… I'm not ready.

"Now, Ro, break the triangle."

Grimacing, she called the elements to her, wishing as hard as she could that they would listen, finding it unsurprisingly difficult. What should have been the air in front of her felt like a firm fabric pushing against her. The elements fizzed past her vision as the triangle sparked, groaning in protest. She felt its fray of electricity stinging her skin.

"Sparrow!"

She could hear the cousins yell, but it seemed like they were further away as she pushed even harder, one hand flat and palm up in front of her until the triangle finally splintered and snapped, leaving her stumbling forward into the dark once more.

She waited, cooling sweat dotting her brow, one arm dangling by her side as she still held the other out. *Was this it?* Ro fought to picture the elements once more, but nothing came to her—just a swampy night. "Guys…? I don't think it worked. Maybe I don't have powers, and this is the sign that we're all wrong about this."

"Ro," Ace called with laughter on his voice. "What do you see?"

"Nothing," she said. "That's my point."

"No, silly."

She felt frustrated. Even Zee was giggling at her.

"Open your eyes, Sparrow."

With a huff she did, gasping with sudden surprise.

Dancing through her finger tips were two of the

elements she had pictured. Yet this time, she could see the proof of them being real. One frozen ice ball spun in front of her, leaving droplets of water on her wrist as bits of rock chased it, scraping her slightly as they went by. She turned her hand, amazed. "Is that…? Am I…?"

"Yes, that's all you, honeybee," Zee chimed.

Ro laughed, watching the graceful movements as she twisted and turned her hand.

"Are you ready for a real spell?" Ace grinned wickedly at her.

"Spell? Isn't that what I'm doing?"

"No, you've just selected the magic that is drawn to you. What you just preformed is a brief part of our selection ceremony. Now that we know you are drawn to earth and ice — "

"Water," Zee corrected.

"Ice, water, same thing."

"Not really," his cousin told him pointedly.

"Anyway. Now that we know you are drawn to those, we know what spells you might be able to use. It's getting pretty late, but I'm going to run one by you just in case we run into more trouble tomorrow. You have a penchant for getting into trouble."

She stuck her tongue out at his jab.

"This will work while you're moving or standing still. It's not particularly strong or needing much precision, but it might help you until we can get you more training. "

"Now, Zee, stand over there." He gestured to a spot five feet behind the fire. "I want you to run toward Ro like you're going to attack her, no spells or anything hardcore, you're a trained militant and she's a civilian, so take it easy."

"Wait she's going to attack me?"

"Oh, don't worry, I wouldn't hurt a precious soul like you." The sultry comment was emphasized by a wink.

Ro didn't know whether to worry or to admit to the blush fighting to creep up her cheeks.

"No, she is not actually going to hurt you, and you're going to protect yourself anyway."

"Right…" Ro eyed up the grinning girl across from her. "And just how do I do that?"

"As she's running toward you, bring both your arms toward your chest and shout *Murus*, then make two fists and jab them into her direction while yelling *Vunus*. Think you can do that?"

"Yeah," she nervously agreed "Vulnus and Murus, vulnus and murus. I've got this"

Zeendria raced toward her, sword drawn inhumanly fast.

Wrong, so wrong. I do not have this… at all. What was the spell again?

She threw her arms out, flat in the night air. *"Murus!"* she cried.

Zee seemed to stumble, but picked herself up quickly.

Wrong, so wrong, she thought as the sword came down upon her.

With wide eyes, Zee froze, the cool metal stopping

just before hitting Ro's skin. "Seeeee? I wouldn't hurt you."

Ro heard Ace sigh. Whether it was from relief or annoyance, she couldn't tell.

"Ace can be a pretty frustrated teacher at times. You'll get it next time," Zee said, answering Ro's unspoken question. She kissed the tip of Ro's nose. "Boop" she said and spun away, bouncing back to her starting spot.

What. Just. Happened?

Another sigh from Ace broke her stunned silence. "It's her first time, Zeendria. There are bound to be mix ups. You, on the other hand, were directed not to use a weapon, and to treat her like a civilian."

"I wasn't going to hurt her, you know that, and now she does too. Besides, if we're being attacked, then they are not going to come at her with sunshine and rainbows, are they? No, they will come at her with spells and weapons. She needs to be properly prepared."

"Yes, but —"

"No buts," she interrupted him.

"She's right, Aceius," Ro said. "Zee, come at me again with the sword. I'll be more prepared this time. What did I do wrong?"

Grumbling, Ace moved beside her. "You're going to want to copy my movements." He brought his fists against himself and then punched them outwards, repeating this a few times. "Murus first, then Vulnus. It's technically two spells in one. You did the wrong move last time. You slowed her down, which is good, but you're looking to stop her completely. Now, let's try this again." He moved to the fire, striking a pose not too different from a military commander. "Again!"

Zee raced toward her once more.

The gleam of the sword strengthened her determination. Ro pulled her fists toward her chest. *"Murus!"* she cried.

In amazement, she watched as Zee's pixie-like body slammed into a thin wall of jagged ice and fell. She grimaced, shooting back to her feet and turning hard as she shoved through the wall.

"Vulnus!" Ro shouted, punching her fist and shooting hard jagged bits of ice that flew toward Zee, one just barely missing her as she fell to the ground, laughing.

"Oh no!" Ro ran toward the girl. "I'm so sorry, are you okay?" She helped her up as a grinning Zee's laughter matched her cousins.

"Am I okay?! Ro, did you see what you just did?!"

"Those spells came from me. That magic came from me."

"Now, that's nothing on someone who is properly trained," Ace said. "But you're already showing incredible strength. You just knocked down one of my best officers."

"Hey!" Zee protested. "I'm not that easy to take down. Get me on the field and you'll see that."

The bickering paused as they looked at Ro. Her face cracked wide with a smile. Now she had hope.

"You okay?" Zee asked

Ro copied Ace's military pose, much to the enjoyment of her friends. "Again!" she said.

It was going to be a long night.

CHAPTER FOURTEEN

The room was warm, but it felt off. Wrong. Almost like it wasn't really there at all.

"Adyra?" Ro whispered, looking around the bright area, but the young archer was nowhere to be found. Wait, why was she calling for Adyra? She was just with Ace and Zee. Confusion clouded her brain. Was she dreaming again? Lucid dreaming maybe? What had happened? Ro tried to walk but found she couldn't move, stuck to the ground where she stood. A door swung open with a bang as it hit the wall. Wood bounced off the stone and into the face of the person behind the young woman who had stormed in.

"How could you do that?" the woman seethed. "He came to you in earnest and you just… just…."

"Rejected his offer." The man sighed, sitting down gracefully as she paced.

"Yes, exactly! I asked one thing of you, Father. Your support, your — "

"Rinna," he cut her off again, gentler his time. "Why don't you sit down. We'll get some tea and talk about this."

"I. Don't. Want. Tea!" The young woman raised her hands and groaned into the sleeves of her robes. She sat down beside him, grabbing his hands. "I love him. I do. So very much. And I know it's unheard of, and never been done before, but we have to face the odds. I need your support in this. The lves will listen to you, they trust you and they trust me."

"Trust is often misguided and easily removed. I cannot support this communion. It's bad business."

"But the child." She placed her hands on her swollen belly.

"Your child," he continued, "will stand tall as the greatest among the Elves. She will be a true legacy, and the people, both Fae and Elves alike — will find no reason to fear her."

"So, what exactly would you have me do?"

"Denounce him." The words struck the air heavier than bricks. "Denounce him as the father. You'll visit your mother's sister for a bit, and when you return, the child will be that of either an arrangement, your choice of course, or a bastard. The people won't fear the prophecy of this child's power and you remain a high standing member of this family and society's high court." Palpable anger raged through the room on a hot wind from an open window and the woman stood tall.

She proceeded calmly. "It has become apparent to me you care more about this prophecy and your legacy in the eyes of the court than your own daughter or granddaughter. If mom were still here—"

"What?" His temper flared. "Do not bring your mother into this. She left us! Remember that before you use your words so carelessly. If she were here, she would know that the decisions I make are for the good of you and this family. And now, that includes your un-born child. You are not to leave your rooms tonight and after Alexander is escorted out of town in the morning, you *will* visit your Aunt Mace until you are ready to re-turn to court"

"You just have it all sorted out, don't you?" she scoffed. "And what of the Faery queen, Father? Or even of Alexander himself? He loves me and they will not give up this child so easily."

"Sometimes, darling, love just isn't enough."

"You're wrong."

He stormed to the door, yanking it open "You will not leave these rooms! I'll take care of the prince and his mother." He glowered at her. "Everybody has a price! And Rinna, you might hate me for this now, but I'm only doing this for your protection. Remember that next time you decide to start a storm." The door slammed behind him, echoing the thunder that danced around the home.

Ro stood frozen to the scene that had played out in front of her. It wasn't the old man's harrowing words, or even the steely determination in the woman's voice. It was her blue glazed eyes, her messy brown locks. Her name.

For the first time in weeks, Ro stared at the eyes of the women she had fought so hard to understand. Ro wanted to reach out, to wrap her arms around the person who had once meant safety to her, to ask a million questions. But she couldn't. She stood as a ghost, knowing this version of her wasn't there, while Rinna, her mother, remained determined, emitting a strength unlike anything her daughter had ever seen from her.

Jerking, Ro's vision flashed purple, and she felt herself being slowly pulled out of the scene that had played before her.

"Mom!" Ro shot up, firelight warming her from nearby. Her heart was pounding.

"Breathe in and out slowly. Come on." Ace was at her side, a calm anger drifting from him as Ro adjusted her position.

"It's late, Queensguard, leave us." The voice of her mother's father called out to them, causing Ro to realize she wasn't fully back at the camp. Instead, she was in a shimmering room of sorts

"Like hell," Ace snapped back.

Across the room, guarded by an ornate wooden desk sat a man she'd never met, a man she felt drawn to. The one she had just seen in her dream, or perhaps she was still asleep. The green leather couch she found herself on didn't feel anything like the tough grassy ground she had fallen asleep on.

August Angelica, her grandfather, stared piercingly at her.

"Is this a dream?" she mumbled, confused.

"No." August said.

"She is under my protection," Ace said. "Something you seem to already know. If you think for one second—"

August lifted his hand, effectively cutting her friend's angry rambling short. "I'm still the leader of this providence, and you're in no position to defy me. I wish to speak to my granddaughter alone."

Ro took in his strong features and greying hair as he sat before her, tall and strong.

August looked just like she had pictured, though she saw things she hadn't expected: the sadness in the his eyes, the tired lines gracing his forehead. He presented a resilient front, but his frown spoke the same language her mom's did after a hard shift at work. It was a look Ro didn't like and she felt bad for this man she knew so little of.

She didn't have a clue what was happening, but she also felt no fear. "Ace," she said, sending a reassuring smile his way. "Please give me a moment with Mr. Angelica. I think I need to speak to him alone as well."

Ace grumbled to himself, crossing his arms and standing as a shield in front of her.

"Sparrow, you don't understand," Ace said. "He summoned you here. I could only come because of the runes I placed around our camp. If I leave, I can't return. Things work differently here."

Ro felt herself falter at his worry.

"Tell her the rest," the cold voice sliced across the room.

Begrudgingly, Ace glared at August before speaking again. "If you ask me to leave, and truly mean it, I won't have a choice in this situation. I'll have to leave. That's not something I'm comfortable with." His eyes pleaded with her to understand, begging Ro not to face this man alone. "Please."

Ro just smiled with understanding. "I will be okay."

Grumbling, he turned to face her grandfather again. "I will leave, but know this." He stalked a few steps closer. "If you lay one finger on her you have violated the treaty between our kinds, and it won't be taken lightly."

"Oh, begone you fairytale," August said. "She will return to herself safe and whole by morning's light."

With a wave of his hand, Ace evaporated in a puff of magenta smoke, leaving Ro and August alone.

Ro steadied her face, refusing to show any emotion.

With slow deliberateness, August stood, towering above her as he walked around to lean on the front of his ornate desk. "Well, Sparrow," he said. "Stand closer to the firelight. Let me get a better look at this granddaughter of mine."

"Ro," she said. "My name is Ro."

How she sounded so calm she would never know. Ro sat with one leg tucked casually underneath her on the arm of the couch. "And I'd rather not. You can though." She nodded to the fire. "Wouldn't mind getting to see the grandfather I never knew existed."

He chuckled lowly at her. "Brave. I'll give you that. Most wouldn't talk to a man of my standing like that."

"Well, most people would just, you know, call and

invite someone over. Not—what did Ace call it again? —'summon someone when they're peacefully sleeping.'"

"Ahh." He raised his finger between them. "We're not just people though, are we, Sparrow? Me, a high standing governing Elf and you, a prophecy, the foretold powerful bridge between the Elven and the Fae."

Her heart stuttered.

"I can see it, you have questions."

"Yes, I have questions. Of course I have questions. Anyone in my case would have questions." She fought to maintain the peaceful nature of her tone.

"Ask away then, you'll find no secrets here."

She didn't trust this promise from the calculating Elf before her. "You're an Elf… so my mom…?"

He sighed, pinching the bridge of his nose. "Rinna really taught you nothing of our kind, did she? I knew your mother was impossible, but not this—"

"Hey!" she interrupted, forgetting her apprehension.

"You do not get to talk about my mother like that, not after what I just saw in my dream. I'm sure she had her reasons for keeping me in the dark, whatever they might be."

"Oh yes, the dream, you called it? Try memory, her memory to be exact. One that wasn't yours to rifle through. Quite rude, I would say. She didn't raise you with manners either, child."

Ro ignored his insult. "Memory? How would I see her memory?"

"With that." He gestured to her rose-covered bracelet.

Only then did she notice it was softly glowing, a warm hue against her skin.

"It was her grandmother's, my mother's, magicked to protect the wearer from harm. You're still connected to her so you could pull certain things from her when necessary. Apparently, that memory was necessary. When I felt you in my memories, or at least in a memory linked to mine, I summoned you here for a talk, something I normally can't do unless you permit it. To the rest of the world you're still asleep with your friends."

Her mind raced to process this.

"To answer your question though, yes, your mother is a full blooded Elf, a descendant from the Elven kingdom, first justice of the governing high court. Or she would be if your idiotic Faerie father hadn't ruined her life."

Though everything should have been a shock, she was struck by one thing. Trying to ignore the sting she asked, "Ruined because she had me?"

"No." He rolled his eyes, his sigh catching her off guard.

"But what I saw in that memory, that was you sending her away because she was pregnant."

"No." His voice dropped. "That was me attempting to get her to see that sending her to her aunt's and denouncing your father as your father was the safest thing for the both of you. I was only trying to protect you both. Sparrow, I know this world seems all magic spells and fun, but it's not. It's very dangerous, especially for you. Elsina should have had you escorted directly to her offices, not traipsing around with your buddies."

"Elsina?"

"Your father's mother, the one who thought the best way to keep you all safe was to send you away." Hatred hid behind his eyes. "Not like you had the strongest magic users as your protectors if you stayed in this realm," he sarcastically ranted, "She not only sent my only daughter away, but you as well, sending you to life amongst the humans, knowing nothing of who you are! Truth is the most powerful magic. I told her that, but did she listen? Of course not. Now you're stumbling into this, your parents were attacked, and you have no knowledge of what lies ahead."

"Attacked?" A shivering fear shot though her once again as she thought of her 19th birthday and the events that befell it. "Like by the Nefarie... like Peri?"

The temperature suddenly dropped drastically as rain pounded outside.

"Yes, the Nefarie attacked them and you," he said. "Accidentally caused your... what did they call it? Amnesia? They sent Peri to pick you up from the hospital when they couldn't capture you. Althea beat him there through. Peri, that disastrous prick, always wanted nothing more than power. Power they offered when he gave up his closest friends."

She shivered unwillingly, remembering Peri's harsh words in the library. How he claimed to get her parents to understand and just wanted to help her understand too. His truth was nothing that she wanted. "I ran to

Peri for help when I realized something was after me."
She eyed the towering Elf once more with suspicion.
"How do I know you're not going to betray me too?"

A smile cracked his stoic expression. "Smart girl.
Okay then, besides the fact that I've done nothing but
offer you explanations, if you need to know whether I'm
out to hurt you, then test me." He held out his hand.
"Touch my arm or take my hand. The contact will be
enough for the bracelet to tell."

Cautiously she leaned forward, praying this wasn't
another attack. She gingerly poked his arm.

He barked out a laugh, startling her. "I don't bite,
Sparrow."

Feeling a bit silly, she laid her hand on his wrist,
waiting for what she thought was inevitable.

Nothing happened.

"So… any sting?" he asked.

"No." She moved away cautiously.

"No sting means no warning. If the bracelet didn't
warn you, then there is no danger from me. I wouldn't
go around telling everyone about that charm though."

She looked down at the silver roses on her wrist.

"Some knowledge is best kept to yourself."

On that note, she agreed.

"You said you'll give me answers," she reminded
him. "How do I know they are true?"

Again, he smiled as if keeping a secret himself.
"That is up to you to decide. I'm willing to wager
though that your so-called friends didn't tell you much
before dragging you through this mess."

"Those are my friends, thank you!" she snapped.

"So loyal, hardheaded like your mother." He smiled a bit wider. "Your so-called friends are forced to follow strict rules. There's only so much they can tell you. Not to mention they have been strategically placed into your life as a form of protection."

"Wha-what?" she stuttered.

"You think it's a coincidence that Adyra happens to have the skills she does and just happened to be your best friend? What about Aceius? No. They were placed into your life as a safeguard against the Nefarie. The boy's family might be friends of your parents, but they were one of the few selected to keep you hidden, and the girl is even worse. You think those were her real parents that you met? Think again. Adyra grew up in an orphanage, with no family. It's thanks to her lack of connections that she was given the mission to protect you. They were all selected and strategically placed into your life."

Ro's heart broke, not for herself, but for friends. Adyra had never let anything slip, but now the crooked man's orphan comment made a lot more sense. It didn't matter though. Even if the relationships were built on false pretenses or half-truths, the moments she had with them, the emotions, those were real, and nothing could change that.

"So?" she pushed back. "I'm sure Adyra had a good reason for not telling me. They're still my friends."

His face softened. She could see more of her mother in him them, kinder eyes, less of the frantic worry and residing pain from a past she would never fully know or understand.

"You've bonded with them," he remarked. "You trust them? Even with your life?"

She nodded, full of determination.

"Good, you'll need that for what's to come."

Soft orange light broke through the room, and he returned to sit behind the desk. "We don't have much longer now. I'll have to send you back." He looked almost regretful, some of that sadness creeping back in.

"Wait." She wanted to prolong the moment, afraid to let go of the closest thing she had to her mother.

"There's just not enough time right now. You have to go."

Ro didn't know what she was expecting. A hug? Some sort of teary goodbye? Anything but this. "Will I see you again?"

"Of course, you're in your rightful world now, child."

"I am not a child."

He motioned for her to calm. "We won't meet again for a while, there's too much you don't know yet to get into the details. Just, Ro? Stay by your friends and hurry to Merwin. I'll do what I can from here to shorten the path. Don't leave the city gates until you know more magic."

She almost snapped back another witty remark, but the orange light obstructed her view, making him seem further away than he really was. "Wait!" she called, but it was too late. The warm glow embraced her senses, lulling her into sleep.

"Sparrow," he called out. "One more thing. Say hello to your mom for me."

With that, she tumbled over the edge, surrounded by peace once more.

CHAPTER FIFTEEN

Sleep stuck to her crusted eyelids as they winced open. Harsh sunlight filtered through the tree line as she sat up, feeling heavy and grimy, probably smelling like campfire smoke and sweat from the dreams. That had been a weird one, but at this point Ro knew better than to question it. Shaking leaves from her hair, she looked down to Ace's lopsided grin. "What?"

"Good morning to you too, sleeping beauty. You look awfully hungover for someone who didn't drink."

"Yeah, well, you don't look too perfect yourself." She straightened out the cracks in her stiff bones.

A muffled shout came from their hunched companion. "Oh god… no…. ugh whyyyyyy does the sun hate me?"

"Zee? You okay there?" Ro called.

"Noooo," Zee uttered, pulling herself up beside

them. "I need coffee. Preferably accompanied by a shower and some surgery goodness."

"She's fine," Ace said, throwing a belted bag at Ro. "She'll be like this until we get closer to Merwin."

"Merwin?" Ro slid the hefty parcel around her waist.

"Yes, Merwin. Ye old kingdom of Faeries, bringers of light and wishes and tinker bells everywhere. Blah blah blah yada yada yada. Merwin."

Zee kicked dirt over the remaining coals. "Can we go now? I don't know about you two, but I really don't want to spend another night sleeping on the forest floor. Unless you mind cuddling with the bugs that is."

"Wait." Ace chuckled as he gestured for her to calm down. "Patience is a virtue. First of all, Ro, do you remember the spells we taught you last night? At least, well enough to use them?

The spells: Murus and Vulnus. How could she forget? Before passing out beside the smouldering heat she had spent the better part of two hours practicing the words over and over as Zee raced toward her, baring that glinting sword. They had practiced until her mouth had gone dry and her muscles protested at the slightest movements. Even now, they pained her as she stretched. Was she comfortable enough to use them though? In a way that they would actually work? "Yes. If I have to use them, I can. Or at least I think I can."

"You can." Ace's smile softened. "You don't have to be perfect, but the Nefarie are not expecting you to have the capability to use any spells at this point. So anything to throw them off their feet the better."

"Right," she nodded. "At least until the two of you show me more."

"Two spells and she's getting cocky, huh?" Zee said.

They moved out and Ro took a spot in the middle of their line as the bouncing pixie behind her muttered, "Oh, thank God…" before pushing them ahead. "ON-WARDS TO THE COFFEE!"

Ro was so caught up in her mind's ramblings she had stopped paying attention to her surroundings. The area around her was pretty hard to ignore though when she found herself slamming into something firm in front of her. Stumbling back, Zee caught her as she held her nose. "Ow, Aceius, What the — ?"

"Shhhh!" he whispered, pulling them both to duck behind some bushes.

"See there?" Zee whispered, eyes focused just above the scraggly vines. "They're dumb as rocks but attracted to sound. You do not want to piss them off."

"Okay, I'll take the back. Both of you walk along the tree line until we are further down the road," Ace instructed and they fell in line.

They ventured ahead, sore bodies protesting the snail's pace. Almost past the goblins, Ro held her breath, stumbling when a loud boom shook the ground.

"You don't think…?" Zee whispered to Ace's sharp look. The earth beneath them shuddered again.

"What?" Ro whisper-yelled, not liking the look that shot between them.

Ace spun her to face him head on. "Ro, when I tell you to, you go. Turn and head along the path."

She glared into his wide eyes, not understanding.

"Merwin isn't too far past that," he explained. "Just go and don't turn around. Zee!"

The other girl jolted to attention.

"Yes, Commander."

"You take the lead and alert the guards at Merwin's gates as to what's coming."

"What's coming?" Ro pushed.

"Where there are goblins, other creatures are never too far behind." Ace drew his longsword, pushing aside the bush in front of him. The trees trembled around them. Laughing manically, the goblins scattered and skipped around the falling rubble.

"Now!" Ace yelled, pushing the two girls ahead.

They took off down the path, legs pumping as trees shuddered and tumbled.

"DRAAAAGOOOON!"

Shards of ice flew around them as the temperature drastically dropped. At the identifying shout, Ro found herself faltering, gawking in awe at the magnificent beast towering over them as it broke onto the forest path. Shades of blue and white curved around its body. The glint of its icy massive wings burned Ro's retinas. It drummed the ground beneath its heavy feet with each pounding step through the forest, and its wide eyes searched out its target, which seemed to be them. Gusts of wind swirled around them as Zee yanked Ro down the path after her. Though she could see Zee's mouth moving, nothing could be heard over the animal's deafening roar.

Glancing back, Ro felt a little relief to see Ace was following close behind them, sword drawn and running backwards. Fire shot out of Zee's hands, and she ran at a breakneck speed, bursting into a clearing.

Ro stumbled up the massive hill in front of them, her back slick with sweat by the time they struggled to the top. Sunny skies and warm temperatures were strange to feel at her front as hail and snow rained down behind her, not to mention the angry roars from the beast she could feel pouncing closer.

"I swear," she yelled at Zee. "If we've come this far just to die at the hands of a dragon…"

Zee's quick burst of laughter brought some sort of relief, and whether it was overdue hysteria or she had finally lost her marbles, Ro felt her face breaking into a wide grin before she tripped over her feet, coming face first with the dirt. Grimacing, she whipped the muck away, turning to quickly stand. Ace ran behind them, not a full gallop, but more of a relaxed and practiced stride, calm in the face of the monster before them. No, she thought, monster wasn't the right word. The dragon was magnificent. Shining and glimmering, angry and shooting daggers of frigid ice their way. It was both glorious and terrifying, yet Ace didn't falter in the path of its destruction. Facing the danger head on, long streams of fire flew from him as he strategically shot fireball after flaming fire ball toward the creature. It was like an elaborate dance, both moving smartly and swiftly around each other.

Ro found herself so entranced in this display of the impossible that she forgot to watch out for herself. Zee was still running ahead, shouting for her to move along, to move out of the way. A steaming, frosted dagger headed for the very spot she stood, and she didn't notice it until it was almost too late. Frost froze her feet to the ground beneath her. Everything else dropped away as she helplessly watched the threat approach.

Ro's body moved of its own accord. Without realizing what she was doing, hands flew against her body and she found her voice. *"MURUS!"* she cried. Power rumbled through her body and out of her open palms as she forced them forward and open. *"VULNUS!"*

Everything exploded.

Rubble flew. The glass dagger aimed for her shattered, bursting into a million iridescent pieces around her.

"Sparrow!"

She turned quickly to find Zee yanking her back over the grassy hill. Her feet were loosened from their frozen state.

"What were you thinking?" Zee asked, panting.

"I did magic." It was all she could muster.

"Yeah, and you could have been killed!"

Up ahead, a tall creamy building rose out of the ocean. Women and men dressed much like the praesidium navigated the land in front of them. Perceiving them as a threat, Ro raised her hands once more.

"Stop!" Zee all but snapped.

A short stout man skidded to a halt.

"Zeendria, ma'am," he said. "Heard you got into some trouble, huh?"

"Oh, nothing we couldn't handle." Zee's charm had returned, and Ro could see she wielded it stronger than any weapon.

"The gates forces are regrouping, and the dragon should be ushered away shortly."

"Thanks for the assist, handsome. Let me just get this one to the gates and we'll see who handles that dragon first, eh?"

They resumed their pace, stumbling through throngs of what Ro could only assume were the guards from Merwin. Or were they the Queensguard too?

"Ushered away?" Ro questioned, gasping for air as they raced up onyx stairs into a high tower.

"What?" Zee barked as they came to a high landing overlooking the scene below as Fae poured out to handle the dragon. "You didn't think we would kill it, did you?"

Ro was just happy to stop for a moment to catch her breath again. "Well, I mean…?"

"Of course not!" The other girl looked shocked. "We're just going to relocate it."

A thick beefy hand clamped down on her shoulder. Sparrow couldn't hide her jump as she followed the arm to a hulking stout man with a grimace on his face.

"This is Gref," Zee said. "You're going to go with him while I handle this dragon business."

"Wait, what?"

"As the missus said, I'm your escort home," he grunted.

"Excuse me?" She shot Zee a wide look.

"Oh, he's harmless, really a big softie. The best one to get you home."

"Home? What home?"

"Ask Gref. It's been fun, Ro."

Sparrow realized how close Zee stood to the edge of the building, the battle behind her.

"You're going back there?" she asked, astounded.

"Well of course, gorgeous." Zee gave a mock salute and a wink that would make a lesser person's knees weak. "Can't let the boys have all the fun, can I?"

With a final grin, she stepped off the landing, whooping as she fell to the ground below.

CHAPTER SIXTEEN

The sky cracked open. Large, jagged hailstones decimated their path as Ro and Gref raced from the fray. Voices boomed and armoured feet clamoured out a clanking tune. Ro gazed out on the chaos, unable to see the dragon through the whiteout it created with each powerful burst of snow from its lungs. They were a safe enough distance away to feel the warmth of the blue sky, but still close enough to feel the rumble of the group setting out to capture the creature.

"Ahem."

Ro spun around.

"Follow me."

Gref growled and Ro ran to catch up with him. His silence sat awkwardly between them for a while.

"You're Gref?"

He responded with a long grunt.

"How do you know Zee?"

Two grunts.

She rushed after his long strides through the bustling city. People, Elves, and Dwarfs alike moved through the buildings and shops. Enticing spices danced in the wind.

"Are they not worried about the dragon?" she asked, astounded that no one seem disturbed by the drop in temperature or the dragon they had encountered."

"Nah, they're used to it. If the creature manages to breach the gates, then an alarm will sound. Until then, they know there's no reason to panic."

"Gref—"

"Gru-ef"

She stumbled into his back as he stopped. "What?"

"My name. It's Gru-ef, not Greef"

"Oh-oh, sorry Gru-ef." She sounded it out just like he was.

"Yes, Domina, just speed it up next time."

Ro's face flushed. "Well, Gref, I am Sparrow not Domina." She could have sworn he smirked under that massive beard.

"Aye," he said, nodding. He moved them toward a darkened walkway that looked like it just barely survived the last storm. Rubbish lay strewn about and the alley carried an odd musk, barely allowing room for two.

"Nah," Ro said, hanging back. "Thanks Gref, but I'll take my chances with the big scary dragon."

His steely gaze met hers. "That thing? It was nothing more than a babe."

"THAT was a baby?!"

He grunted again. "They entrusted you to me, Domina. We will take the back roads." He yanked her hood up. "You are to stay hidden until we get you to safety."

"My name is Sparrow, GRU-EF. Not Domina. Are we not safe here? In Merwin?"

"Even the tallest guard towers lack the ability to ensure no traitors lay in their mist."

She rushed down the path to his side. "Oh yeah?" she said. "And why should I trust you?"

"Do you trust your friends?"

"Well… yes," she admitted begrudgingly.

"Then trust that they have entrusted you to me."

They continued walking, the path long and quiet, her boots catching each puddle.

Even with the high sun she shivered in the cold.

"Here," he said.

They turned out of the alley. A wide, barren market and shuttered shops presented themselves.

"It's so quiet," Ro said. "Where is everyone?"

"We're in the school district. The Halls of Ivy are this way. Come spring, this portion of the city is as bubbling as any other."

"Ace mentioned the school, it's a school, right?"

They continued, past darkened buildings as Gref chuckled. "Schooling here is a bit different than on the mortal plain. As an adolescent, you train for years, honing your skills. Leading to a selection ceremony."

"Selection ceremony?"

"Up until then, young ones are trained in elements, science, creative arts, and general magic. During the ceremony, the student will select the path that draws them in, that calls to them as a passion."

"So, Adyra and Ace did this?"

"Yes, they both attended. Just a few streets over from where we are now, where you should've gone, in my opinion."

Ro strained, looking for any type of school building that would be along the way.

"Don't bother, Domina, you cannot see it from here. Perhaps one day you'll visit, but not today."

"Why do you call me that?" she muttered as they continued.

"Lady."

"What?"

"It means lady in the olden tongue. A form of respect."

"Oh, Gref, I—"

"Oh, for the mother of the Gods. When did she change the shops hours?" The giant bouldering Elf seemed exasperated as he stumbled to a stop outside a building that shimmered duskily as people milled in and out of the sparkling shop door.

"What's that place?" she asked, the store showcasing a bronze façade in stark comparison to the grey buildings around her.

"Keep moving," Gref ordered.

She couldn't though. The shop stood shining and singing, calling to her.

"Sparrow, no."

"But—"

"No, I am on strict orders to escort you to the estate, not to some magic shop. It was supposed to be closed today anyway." He reached out to pull her arm.

"Listen, big dude, I'm going to level with you here. I don't really have much say over anything else in my life right now and probably won't for a while."

He faltered. "You are your own person, you will always have a say."

A deep sigh left her body as she turned to look up at his towering height. "This is the first chance I could see a magic shop here, and I am about one hundred percent sure it will be nothing like the ones where I am from." Her first taste of magic had been exhilarating, leaving her wanting more. "Maybe this will help me understand it a bit more. Just a quick pop in and we will be on our way. No one needs to know, please?"

Sure, the guilt was laid on pretty thickly, but he seemed to get the point, the roll of his bushy brows turned to a grin. "One look-see and then we're out of here."

Joy coursed through her, and Ro beamed before rushing inside the shimmering building. Cool air met her at the door as she gazed around in amazement at all the dancing assortments in the shop. Books lined up and rotated themselves in a graceful display along the walls, begging her to reach for them before she got distracted by a little wooden bird flittering around the room. She laughed as Gref shuffled beside her.

He grunted and walked over to a display of shaking

chocolates as she found herself wandering over to a wide case of levitating rocks. Each one a little bit different, she held her hand out to them, mesmerized as they rotated softly around her fingers. Each curved edge shining in the light.

"Careful there, dear." Ro jumped at a smooth, feminine voice behind her. "Each gem is destined to guide you in opposite ways."

Yanking her hand from the case, Ro turned to the woman.

"A little agate for balance and protection, some amethyst to calm your nerves. Fluorite for when you need a little more insight."

"I'm sorry, I just have never…" Ro couldn't find the words. If this was common, then it would have been suspicious that she had stood so entranced by them.

"First times are freewill to everyone, child." The women glided over, winking with knowing eyes.

"Oh," Ro blushed "First time? I'm —"

"Our secret, don't worry." Her chuckle was musical, accompanying Gref's footsteps until he was beside Ro once more.

"Oh," the woman gleamed. "Greffuld, dear, I didn't expect to see you today. Playing tour guide?"

"Esmeralda, no need to stir up drama here" retorted the mountainous beard. "That's our cue to leave." His hand landed squarely on Ro's shoulder, and she glanced between them.

"Oh, but you mustn't leave yet!" The thin tall women floated closer. "I am Esmeralda Gaslentstonian," she gestured to herself. "It's very nice to finally meet you, Sparrow. I understand your journey here has been hard, but…" her smokey irises danced toward Gref playfully, "…if you will allow me a moment of your time, I believe you lost something along the way. With just a simple sight trip—"

"We're leaving" Gref insisted.

"Wait, ho-how did you know my name?"

"She's a sight-giver, Sparrow," Gref explained. "One that we are not dealing with now. My job is to get you home safely. Not to allow you to be derailed by some glitzy hack."

The sight-giver's tinkling laugh flitted in between her words. "Oh Gref, darling, you don't mean that! Keep it up and I will just have to let lovely Ryan know that his husband's been spoiling all my fun. Now I know it's a lot to take in, why don't you two take a moment and talk it over, but Sparrow dear, do remember, it's your life, thus your decision." She led them away.

It wasn't until they were almost to the door that Ro even processed the conversation. "It's Ro!" she called back with a smile. "My friends call me Ro."

She stopped at the front of the shop. "Gref, I want to do it. You know her, right?"

His eyes popped wide.

"She's a fake," he sputtered.

"Fake, huh? Are you willing to vouch for that? After all, isn't she your friend? She obviously knows you and your husband."

"Stupid Emmie and her big mouth."

"Emmie?" She interrupted the fountain of grumbles.

"Okay, girl."

"Ro."

He sighed in exasperation "One sight trip. One. Then we leave. In and out, quick and easy, and no one knows about this. No one. Understood?"

"Great, one sight trip coming right up," Esmeralda announced, suddenly beside them. She smiled as the open sign flipped itself to close. "Come on, come on." She ushered them toward the hallway behind the counter. "We don't have all day, darlings. One sight trip coming right up."

They followed the small hallway, ducking under a low door frame. The room was bone-chillingly cold, Ro realized, as damp stone walls greeted them.

"Hmph" Gref muttered, his large shoulders making the space more claustrophobic.

"Well, sit down you two!" The thin lady flitted around them. Two chairs scraped the floor as they moved themselves into upright positions around a small table.

Ro sat gingerly, squinting to see Esmeralda knocking dusty bottles around in the darkness. Groaning, the older guard collapsed into the chair that was too small for him, his bent knees almost to his chin in the tiny space.

Laughter fought to bubble from her lungs. Not at him, of course, but at the situation. Here she was, waiting to see some sort of destiny in what looked to be a rundown broom closet. Or at least she would have laughed, had the stink not hit her first. Slightly acidic and deeply rotten, it launched onto her nose and traversed her taste buds.

"Oh… oh no… what is that?" came her gagged question.

"I told you. Bad idea." But there was laughter in Gref's eyes.

"Oh, just ignore it, darling, you'll be used to it soon enough." Esmeralda sat between them. She carefully held a curvy glass vial. The purple smoke that bubbled out of it seemed to hold the stench.

"Is that…?"

Her voice all but sung in response. "Sorry about the state of the room. These things are best hidden. You see, not a lot of people can understand that knowing the possibilities of the future is not always for everyone." Her hand gave Ro's a quick squeeze. "The smell on the other hand…" The vial dance between her fingers. "Well, you didn't think that all potions smelled like kittens and rainbows did you, dear? Ha! I wish. A crushed dragon's scale mixed with mud root will leave a scent you can't get rid of for days. Lucky for us, there's none of that in here." She beamed at them. "Now, Sparrow, hand out and palm down. There's no time to dillydally."

Nervously, Ro moved her hand to the centre of the small table. Hovering just above the wooden surface, she fought not to have it shake. What if this was a mistake? Gref himself had warned against it… but one look at the muttering man showed he was anything but wary of danger in that moment.

The vibrant liquid slowly shook, tumbling downward. Ro jumped as it hit her skin, watching the bubbles expand, popping slowly behind her fingers and diving around her thumb.

"GRATI FIANT OCULIS MEIS. VISUS FORTITUDINEM MEAM. VOLUNTARIE REVELATIONI!"

The room swirled. Dusty and darkened walls spinning together to pull visions of colour around them. Sparks of green, yellow, and red danced around voices calling her name.

"Sparrow…Sparrow… Ro!" Gref pulled her attention toward Esmeralda once more. "Ignore everything else but her!" he told the girl. The table in the middle lifted a few inches off the ground, rapidly spinning.

The seer's eyes locked with Ro's once more. An entire galaxy pulled her into its bright stars and glowing orbs within her gaze.

"Three paths lay ahead," Esmeralda said. "One is broken, one fights dread. One falls ahead. Trip upwards to find strength."

Everything stopped. The table slammed back into place. A putrid smell still lingered as the dripping of water on stone returned. "Here, dear."

Ro found her hands suddenly full, stomach shaky, eyes tired. She lifted the cup to her lips and the lukewarm drink lingered bitterly in her throat as she swallowed.

"Drink up, darling, seeing your future is never fun." Esmeralda glided them out of the closet space.

"See?" Ro found herself sputtering. "I didn't see

anything. Just your eyes going all spacey. What exactly was I supposed to see?"

"Hey now," Gref cut in between their standoff. "This isn't some fantasy flick, you hear me? Esmeralda here saw your future for you. What you take of it is your own choice. That's why she doesn't run this business very much, too many people upset over misunderstood answers."

"You said she was a fake."

"I was trying to get you to leave the shop."

A sigh escaped her as they reached the front room again. The lights were still off and sign still flipped, signalling an empty nest. "I'm sorry. I recognize this is a risk that you have taken for me."

Esmeralda's hand slid down Ro's crossed arms comfortably. "A risk I will always be willing to take for you, my dear"

It was a sweet gesture but did nothing to calm her ailing nerves.

"Did you see anything? About me I mean?"

"What I receive are just flashes. Bits of colour but no clear picture. Almost like watching an old grainy movie, but the audio doesn't quite match up with the pictures, you know? Give me just a moment." She stood tall, still partially in the hallway.

It wasn't quite like what Ro had expected. No weird shouting or eyes rolling to the back of Esmeralda's head. The older woman stood perfectly still, the evening light flickering over her closed eyes as she squinted in concentration. Just as Ro went to make sure she was alright, Esmerelda spoke. Her words chilling to the bone.

"You will make the right decision. This I know for sure. No matter what path you choose, it won't fulfill you, won't make you happy. There will continue to be something missing, a slight unease set between your brows. The one who presents themselves as the most caring, wraps their poisonous daggers in the most becoming cloth of trust. This person lies in the future ahead of you. No matter where you go, you are destined to meet. And no matter what choice you make, which of the three paths you choose, you will always be the girl spliced with grey. Even surrounded by loved ones you will continue to be the girl forever alone. One path stands stormy, another just filled with clouds. The last painfully blinding. The choice is yours."

Sadness washed over her. No, this was heavier than sadness, yet more unfeeling than despair. She was numb, cold, helpless. Nodding, she took a deep breath in. When Esmerelda opened her eyes, it was with a look of finality. There was nothing more she could tell them.

"We can go now, Gref. Thank you, Esmeralda." She turned to leave.

"Now wait here, missy," Gref said sternly. "Esmerelda went out of her way to help you just now."

She paced her words calmly. "I am grateful. I don't know who this person is you are describing me meeting, but based on your words, it doesn't matter. It sounds like I'm screwed either way. All paths."

Her companions shared a glance.

"I'm going to go out on a limb here and assume this has something to do with either staying here after I find my parents, or returning home. No matter what, it ends up with me being alone. And Gref," her wet blue eyes peered through him, "I'm tired. So tired of not knowing what's going on, of people hiding things from me. Of being scared and even of being angry. I'm so tired of being alone."

"You're not alone, Sparrow. You have Adyra and Zee—"

"Yes, but she got one thing right, don't you see? Even when I am surrounded by friends, hell, even when I had my parents, I was still alone. Or lonely at least."

"So what? You're just going to leave now? Give up after all—"

"I'm not giving up." Her sigh deflated her whole body. "We'll go straight to the meeting point. I will find out what happened to my parents, and I will survive this, Gref. I'm giving in."

"Or," Esmeralda's quiet voice cut in with a soft smile, "you could choose a different path."

"But you just said that either path I choose are basically not great."

"What if one of those paths is a mixture of both? Another better option? Figure out what that is for you."

CHAPTER SEVENTEEN

They continued along paths and alleyways, their silence speaking volumes, as their footsteps reverberated off the cobblestone. Every step made Ro more and more determined to forge her own path, uninfluenced. But that would be impossible. Everyone was influenced by everyone else: by what they did and what they said. Yet she refused to be controlled by anything else anymore. Yes, the world wasn't black and white, but all she needed was to ensure her family was safe, get answers of her own, and then she would make a logical decision based on facts—not emotion—on what the best path for her was. First, she would need some answers. How to know if she could trust the person she was asking though…? Then it hit her and she froze.

"Sparrow?" Gref halted beside her. "You okay, kid?"

She turned slowly. "Can I see your hand, please?"

"What…?" he sputtered.

"Your hand. Let me see it, please."

Cautiously, he held out his hairy palm.

Ro lifted her arm and rested her wrist with the rose bracelet in his hand. "Come on… come on."

Nothing happened. She tried again, rolling her hand around his arm. She was told the bracelet would give her a warning against those who meant to harm her in some way. Sure, it wasn't perfectly tested, but if her theory was correct, her arm should be stinging or burning right now. Much like it had when she hugged Peri.

"Uh, kid?. You alright there?

She huffed, rolling it around again. Still nothing.

Casting a blinding smile in his direction she chimed, "Just testing something. How far away are we?"

"Only another ten minutes or so."

"Well, come on then." She moved forward, letting him lead them once more. "Hey Gref…." she spoke over his confused grumbles. "Can I ask you some questions?"

"Sure. Can't say I'll answer them all, but whaddya got?"

"Well… how exactly do you know Zee?"

"Zeendria is a spitfire. She burst through the captain's ranks, topping that of even her cousin."

"And Ace?"

"Yeah, that boy went more into politics, family requirement, I'm sure. Zeendria on the other hand, no one could tell her what to do. You put her and Adyra together and they're more mischievous than any other could take on. I'm pretty sure the school still has some marks from some odd prank or potion they made."

"Hmm… and you… you trust them?"

"With my life." His answer was firm, unwavering as they walked.

"And the Nefarie?" She let the question hang.

"Oh, those blubbering idiots…" She practically felt his eye roll. "A bunch of fools who think that worlds should have never been divided. Hoping to use you to bring them back together and give the mortals payback for pushing us out. Idiocracy, I tell you. Mortals had a right to fear magic they could never understand. Our side was not perfect either. But the way it is now avoids bloodshed."

"Wait, hold on. That's what I don't get. How am I, someone who didn't even know magic existed before now, supposed to help them bring the worlds together?"

"Extremists get crazy ideas stuck in their head. Your parents splitting to the mortal world didn't help."

"Way to give me the answer without actually giving me the answer there, Greffie."

He shrugged. "Wish I could tell ya more, kiddo, but honestly, I don't know. Stupid only speaks to stupid."

She could hear the noise of a crowd now, perhaps a few streets over.

"Do you know why I was brought to Merwin?"

"Oh, that's an easy one." They turned into a plaza that was swarming with Fae. They milled about shops —eating, talking, laughing—their skin an array of green, red, and purple, and Ro fought hard not to stare in amazement.

They pushed through the crowd, heads down under their heavy hoods. "You're here to see your grandmother," Gref said.

"What?"

"Grandmother, and parents of course."

"Wait, my parents are here?"

"Geesh, they really didn't tell you anything, did they?"

"Nope," she popped sarcastically. "Are they okay? My parents, I mean? And grandmother? Which one? She lives here or…?"

"Yes, she lives here, you'll see them all soon, kid."

They continued walking through the busy streets. *That would make two new grandparents in one day,* Ro thought. As they walked, she found she kind of liked the bumbling, grumbling giant who escorted her. Sure, he was rough around the edges, but he wasn't all that bad.

Unfortunately, just when she was starting to get comfortable, he threw another wrench in her plans. "Here we go. I told you it was only a stone's throw." Gref nodded at the ornate guard towers as they passed them.

She felt like someone had doused her in cold water. "Hold up, I thought you were taking me to my grandmother?"

A towering estate sprawled in front of them. Almost castle-like. Gref pounded on the door.

"This is your grandmother's home, Domina."

"This the girl, Gref?" An ostentatious guard, fitted in the same uniform she had seen those at the gate wearing, peeled the door open when Gref nodded.

"Come on, Ro, and good day, sir." He ushered her past the questioning guard and into the tower walls. Sandstone and agate danced along the stone as he led her to a blue elevator. "Sparrow, this is where I leave you"

"Wha-what?"

He pushed a button beside her. "This elevator only has one stop. It will open to your rooms. Hold your hand against the door and recite your name. It's been charmed to give you entry."

"Hold on, you're just leaving?"

"I have to check into my post, kid. Besides, these walls are as safe as you can get. You'll see everyone soon." The door opened and he shuffled her into the small rectangular box.

"Wait, Gref. Where will your post be?" She turned around, only to see he was no longer there. The doors closed on her view.

Ro dreaded silence and being alone, something bad seemed to happen whenever she was. Expecting the slow shaky dinging ride of elevators back home, Ro found herself surprised when it shot up. Her ears popped as she held on to a mirrored railing to steady herself. The door quickly opened with a metal clink. That had to be the fastest elevator ride of her life.

Ro stepped out, cautiously and slowly, but found

herself in a softly lit room that held nothing but a door. With anticipation, she pressed her hand to the door, remembering Gref's parting words. "Sparrow Valencia."

The door opened into a room like no other. Black and red colouring took up much of the decor. There was a huge bay window, like one she aways dreamed of sitting and reading at, yet she was unable to see out of it thanks to some sort of misty tint. Ro called out to see if anyone was there, searching throughout the bedroom and small sitting area before finding a letter upon her pillow. The note had elegant sprawling handwriting that she did not recognize.

My dearest granddaughter,

I know this must be confusing. I am tied up for a bit and won't be able to meet you until tonight. Please join me for dinner as we will discuss your parents. I am sorry for the mystery but will tell you anything and everything you wish to know. I have left some fresh clothes in the closet for you, and anything else you might be wanting. We have much to speak about and I look forward to meeting you for the very first time.

Much love,
E.

And so, that's how, an hour later, she found herself stepping out of a bath and gazing into a steamy mirror. Ro thought she would look older, wiser, maybe just a little bit more mystical. Yet the same eyes, nose, and face of the girl she left behind on Claudaith Island gazed back wearily. Water dripped from her hair as she took a few calming breaths. Ten seconds in, ten seconds out. She skimmed the marble counter, filled with tiny bottles. None looked even the slightest bit familiar. Slightly annoyed, she searched until one of the many drawers revealed a brush. Running it through her tangled strands she grabbed the towel and slowly walked toward the bed.

"Hello? Anyone mysteriously show up when I was showering? No? No one?" She opened the closet, pulling out the only outfit that hung there.

"Figures." She blew out a puff of air as she slipped into the one piece. At first glance it looked to be a dress, a long sleeved off-the-shoulder top with a long skirt, but she realized the skirt opened in the front, revealing warm leggings.

Collapsing on the huge canopy bed, she sighed. This whole thing felt like a fever dream. But she was ready for some answers. Rereading the note, she twisted a strand of her hair into a braid, wrapping it around the rest to control the frizz, when two loud knocks resounded from the doors.

"Come in." She stood beside the bed nervously.

Three knocks this time, only faster.

"Come in!" Didn't her grandmother know how to open a door? Knocks resounded even louder this time, more frantic. With a huff, Ro swallowed her anxiety and hurried over, yanking it open.

She stumbled backwards as a ball of bubbling energy wrapped around her.

"You're okay! You're truly positively okay! Oh, I
almost didn't believe it when they told me you were
here, but then I thought, of course she's here. You're
finally truly home! YAY!"

"Whoa... Adyra," Ro spoke over the other girl's
squeals. "What are you doing here? I mean, not that I'm
not happy to see you, but I thought for sure you were...
well, anyone else."

"Though you might like some company. Besides,"
she led them to some chairs. "I told you back in Aylee
that I would answer your questions when I could. Now
that you're safe, I figured I could help, or at least provide some company."

Ro looked at the girl, still holding her hand. She
pulled away, allowing the bracelet to brush Adyra's
palm. Nothing happened.

After a moment of silence, Adyra sighed. "I can't
speak for the others, but I can speak for myself.
Sparrow, please." Her eyes begged.

Ro looking her up and down. "How old are you?"
she asked.

"Don't freak out.... buuuut just shy of 172."

"And you're an...?" She faltered over the word.

"I am part of the Praesidium. I became an archer
shortly after graduation. It takes decades of learning,
honing your skills. You were my first legit mission."

Ro stiffened. "And that's all I was? Just your mission?"

"No, no, that's not what I meant." Adyra sighed. "At

first, yes, it was just a mission. I'm pretty sure they only gave it to me because I had no connections, no family here. It was long term. I had to move in next to you and do status checks until your 19th birthday. We weren't even really supposed to have contact. Ace didn't want anyone he couldn't trust near you; you were never just a job for him. You two did truly grow up together, and he was ready to end any threats to your or your family's safety. We thought the same of his family, but you know what happened with that."

Ro straightened up, hurt but holding back, trying to give Adyra the chance to speak her piece.

"So yes. In the beginning, you were just an assignment. Someone I observed and supported from afar. Do you know what happened then?" She chuckled to herself. "I walked into that classroom alone, ready to observe. No one approached me or sat with me at lunch, but I was okay because that was the job. I was meant to be a loner, to be on the outside, invisible. Then you walked right up to me and started spouting random facts." She laughed this time, imitating Ro with a finger in the air. "Moons' moons are called moon moons. Bananas can't reproduce, and if I remember correctly... it is impossible —"

"—to hum while holding your breath," they finished together.

"Well, yeah," Ro said. "You looked so lonely and out of place. I thought you might need a friend, or at least I thought that's what we were. Friends."

"Ro, we are though. Don't you get it? Before that

moment, I didn't understand friends, or even relationships. I had rivals that I admired in school, sure, but I had no one in my corner the way you were willing to be. You showed me what it meant to truly care for someone, to want to support them in any way, you showed me what true connection was and why relationships are important. You are my friend."

"Then why didn't you tell me any of this?"

"I couldn't. When I graduated, I signed my orders with an oath that while I was within the bounds of the mission, I could not release any of this information to you. There were times when I wished I could. Ace and I argued numerous times with your parents that you had a right to know the truth about your lineage. They refused to change our orders though, and if we broke them, it meant death."

"And after the accident?"

Adyra looked at her sadly. "You know by now the accident was an attack by the Nefarie. We got to you as fast as we could, but there was nothing to be done. They were sent here, and you went with Althea for safety."

Dread rushed through her. "Althea? Is she alright? Peri mentioned talking to her."

"She's fine! She's here. I think she's meant to join you later on."

"Good."

"You were asking about the attack… why I couldn't tell you then?"

"Well, yes. Surely that would have changed the bounds of your contract, right?"

"Nope. My orders were until your birthday. In fact, we were given strict directives not to contact you at all while you were on Claudaith. Only Althea could for your safety."

"The happy birthday text though?"

She looked sheepish. "Technically, my orders expired on your birthday. You turned 19, I couldn't just ignore it."

"Ace did."

"Cut the guy some slack. He follows orders to a capital T. Especially if they involve your safety."

"Why is my 19th so important?"

"That's normally when one fully comes into their powers and discovers what elements they can draw upon."

"Yeah… I did some magic actually."

"What!?"

"Yeah, during the dragon attack. Zee showed me." She caught the other girl's blush. "In the sake of friendship…" Ro rolled back with a smirk. "Are you two, like, together together or…?"

Adyra's blush deepened. "We're friends. Zee is someone I met in school but didn't really get along with at first. We get along now, better than most."

"I think you liiike her."

"I'm not saying I don't." She grinned. "I am saying that our jobs require both of us to be gone for very long times, so while we do check in, we have an agreement that while we're on missions, things aren't so serious. When we have the chances though… yes, you could say we're together."

"I like her… I get the sense she really cares for you too."

"Yeah, well, there's nothing we can do to be together more long term now."

"Gref mentioned marks on the building or some damage to the school."

"Oh, yes." Adyra's booming laugh bubbled out, bringing a smile to Ro's face. "Remind me to tell you about our adventures sometime, you'd get a kick out of them. So, what elements presented to you?"

Ro closed her eyes, slowly pushing her palms out from her chest. Trying to picture the two elements she had called to her in a dark room. Feeling a tingle shivering down her arms and pouring from her centre, Ro opened her eyes at Adyra's gasp.

"Water," she said as droplets danced in a stream between her fingers. "And earth." Grainy rocks shook dirt from their crevices as they formed prisms in her outstretched palm.

"Cool! I pegged you as more of a fire and earth girl."

Quickly, and with much more ease, Adyra did the same. With an air of grace, she glided her hands in between them. Suddenly, a small flame blazed strong above her friend's fingers, wind dancing and pulling it in circles.

They leaned closer to one another.

"You seem to have the air and fire down," Ro said.

Ro suddenly felt weird, like Adyra's flame was calling to her, beckoning her. She moved her floating rocks and water even closer. Water danced on the air, drawing out more from its molecules. Freezing and unfreezing rapidly.

"I've never seen this happen…" Adyra muttered. "Your elements… It's like they want to combine with mine."

Both girls sat mesmerized, moving their hands closer and closer. A spark jumped, Adyra's flame engulfing the rock floating between them. Power surged through both their veins—potent untapped energy unlike anything they had felt before. Gasping, their eyes shot open. The exhilaration Ro felt to the magic she performed had nothing on this. It was pure bliss. They jumped out of their seats in shock. "Is that… is that normal?" Ro asked

"Not that I know of. Did you feel that too?" Adyra asked before they were interrupted as knuckles rapped on the door.

Adyra nodded her head in that direction.

"You're the only one who can open that door. It's a safety charm. You better answer it."

"Right…" Ro walked away from her. "We're trying that again though."

"Agreed."

More knocks sounded across the room.

"Alright, alright. I'm coming. Hold your horses." She pulled the heavy door open once more.

"I haven't seen any horses here… but let me know if you do." Ace stood there in full leather armour, contrasting against the flowerier outfits of both girls. With a second look, Ro noticed Adyra's leather top and the small folded bow attached to her hip. How she had missed a big wooden stick and string she would never know. "Well, hello to you too, please do come in." She bowed sarcastically.

"Why, thank you!"

He stepped closer, conspiratorially. "But I thought I would take you to meet your grandmother."

"Why didn't she come get me herself?"

He shrugged. "I think she'd rather meet you with your parents."

"Wait. Now?"

He nodded.

"Well then, what are we waiting for? Come on, let's go."

They both laughed at her, and they approached the elevator together.

As the azure doors slid shut once more, Ace broke the silence "So are you two…?"

"Yeah," Ro smiled. "I think we're good."

"And are we?" he murmured nervously.

"Look, I'm not saying you don't have some trust to rebuild with me, but I think we're good. We all are okay." With that, tension seemed to break, and they all stood a bit lighter.

"This way," Ace said as they stepped out of the elevator and turned down a long corridor.

"There's one thing you should know before we get there though."

Ro's heart dropped. "Yes?"

"Ace, maybe we shouldn't, it's just speculation," Adyra said.

"No, I'm done hiding things from her. You are too."

They took a few more turns, walking deeper into the massive building.

"What's going on?" Ro tried not to sound impatient or frustrated again.

"Ro… No one has actually seen your parents since they have arrived. They are in the healer's medical rooms, that I know, but they have not made an appearance."

"Now, that doesn't mean that anything bad is going on," Adyra offered. "But… well, they are nobles, and without them making an appearance, the court and house seats have become sort of restless. Your grandmother has been very hush-hush about their status. So… there might be pressure on you to present yourself in their footsteps."

"Wait…" They halted in front of two golden, sandstone doors. "They're nobles? I'm a noble? How would I present myself?"

"Too late, we're here." Ace pushed the giant doors open, directing them inside. "Don't worry, Sparrow. You've got this. "

CHAPTER EIGHTEEN

he room was dim and peaceful. A tranquil waterfall stood in the middle, and cloth-lined beds lined the left wall. Walking slowly past the rows of empty beds hidden behind sheer curtains, Ro noticed a group in the back. Men and women dressed in blue and moving about with purpose. Two figures lay in beds, side by side, but unmoving. Her parents.

Rushing to their sides, her heart leapt to her throat. Finally, she was with them, they were safe. "Mom!" She crouched between them. "Dad!" She tried to shake them gently, but they lay unmoving, seemly asleep, their chests gently rising with each new breath.

"It's the coma…" a nurse started.

A gruff looking older woman in green rose from her spot beside Ro's mom. "Thank you, Anna. I think I can help explain. General. Captain. I see you have brought my granddaughter safely as requested."

Ro waited as both her friends dropped to one knee, brining their hands to lay over their bent knee.

"Of course, my queen. R—Sparrow I mean—is in good health and has been lightly debriefed."

"Oh, none of that," the woman scoffed. "Your family has been good to mine, Aceius, and you both have been good to my granddaughter. No need for formalities. We're all friends here. Now…" She glided to the opposite side of the bed. "Sparrow… my granddaughter… It's so good to have you home at last."

Granddaughter… Queen… Ro found herself crushed in a powerful hug.

"Wait…" She pulled away. "You're… but I'm… you're mistaken. Sorry Mrs… Queen… your highness…"

"Are these your parents?"

"Well…" Ro looked at their still forms once more. "Yes."

"And this right here—" the queen gestured to Ro's dad, moving hair from his face, "is my only son. Prince of the high Fae court, counsellor of the high Elven realms. That makes you my granddaughter."

Ro felt like she had been slapped in the face or taken a plunge into freezing water. Yes, she had been given these facts, but actually seeing her parents here, meeting two grandparents, it was a bit overwhelming.

She could push that away to process later though, there were more important things.

"Queen…"

"Elsina…You might not be conformable calling me

Nona, or Grandma, but at least use my first name. Not some flimsy title."

"Okay…" Ro gulped. "Elsina… it's nice to meet you." She held out her hand, bracelet dangling. As Elsina shook it, she made sure to let the bracelet bounce between their wrists.

Either the bracelet was no longer working or Elsina meant her no true harm, Ro decided. "That's… a lot to process. Six months ago, I was a girl with no family other than these two, and now, yeah, a lot to process. Could you tell me what's wrong with them?"

"Well…" Her grandmother sat on the edge of her son's bed. "I was hoping you could help with that."

"Me? How?"

"We know the Nefarie found you and your parents. In doing so, they knocked your parents into a coma, a bit like the coma you were in. Seeing as you were not the main target, the curse they used didn't linger with you as long, but it seems to have some lasting effects."

Ro nodded. "I can't remember the attack. Or anything about it."

"If you'll come with me? I know I invited you to a dinner, and there's some other people who would love to meet you, but first I would love to see if I could help you regain your memories." She rose, extending her hand.

Ro found herself doubtful. "Will they be okay?"

"Oh yes, dear. They are in good health. Just asleep and refusing to wake. The medical unit here continually monitors them and hopefully we can regain something from your memories."

"I'll be back," Ro whispered to the prone figures. Touching them both on the shoulder then following after her grandmother with haste.

"We'll meet you at dinner," Ace said as they passed.

"Yes, you will, Aceius. Both of you are to join us tonight. We need to discuss Sparrow's training if she chooses to stay." Elsina grinned at her on the way out the door. "Oh, and Captain…"

Ace turned.

"Thank you for the report on your family. I will have the everyone briefed first thing in the morning. I know it wasn't easy and I appreciate your selflessness and dedication."

Ro faltered, looking at him in surprise and concern.

"Go," he mouthed with a small sad smile.

She did, walking side by side with Elsina throughout the many corridors and stairways. "I don't know how you don't get lost in this maze," Ro muttered, surprised when her grandmother broke out in guffawing laughter.

"I know. I told Breenus when we first came to this world that nothing so sprawling was needed, but he insisted. And considering it was once of his last requests, a maze we did make."

Ro stumbled in shock. "You and Breenus were the ones who created this world when magic became too much for mortals?"

"Yes, we could use our powers combined, him drawing off of my magic to shape this world. It proved too much for him though, too draining. I know you haven't started your lessons yet but that's an important one. Magic always has a price. The more you use it, the more of your soul it will take. While the soul might be regenerative, if you take too much, like is often done in use of dark magic, then you will lose too much of your soul, and your life span — maybe more — will suffer."

"So, creating this world… it was dark magic?"

"Who's to say what's good or bad?"

They took a few more turns and passed a living room area, the fire roaring in the enclosed space. "What was it like? If you don't mind me asking…"

"The power?" Elsina looked down at her with a smirk. "Like nothing I ever felt before. A sparking energy coursing through me. Only he could access the magic, but I could feel it igniting in my veins, combining with his." They came to another room, this time with an open doorway. "We knew he could activate my powers when both our eyes burned blue with lighting. Haven't seen anything like it since."

Ro paused, this was all fleetingly familiar. Not trusting Elsina enough yet to share, she promised herself she would talk to Adyra later. Speeding up, she halted with her grandmother in front of a giant circular cloud. It rolled into itself, over and over, hovering and misty above a stone pillar.

"What is it?" she asked.

"It's what we are going to use to help you to remember. If it works, that is. It's still kind of experimental."

Ro looked at her in alarm.

"Experimental but safe, it won't hurt you, worst

case scenario is it will do nothing at all."

"So, what do I do?"

"Lay under the cloud. It may feel like it's raining on you, but keep your eyes closed. Think about your parents, about the holes in your memory. It's that simple. I'll be right here." Elsina stepped a few paces back.

Nervously, Ro did as she asked. Taking a deep breath, she placed her body under the mist. It was cold and, wet, dew catching on her lips and eyes. Squeezing them closed, she focused only on the attack and the blackness stopping her from remembering that day. Ro forced herself to breathe. In two three four, out two three four. In two three four. Out, two, three four. Her face relaxed. Trancelike and peaceful, one more breath and she was gone.

Ro knew she wasn't actually gone. She was still laying in Merwin, her body under a drizzling cloud. She could still feel the wet air. Yet for the life of her she would have bet anything that she was sitting in her room, happy to be almost done with chores. It was light and airy, the sun shining bright through her windows. Adyra would be over soon for the cookout, Ace and his parents too. Her dad had gotten a new smart grill. He could monitor the temperature and settings for the brisket he was smoking from the comfort of the couch where he had planted himself for the rest of the day.

She was folding clothes at the end of her bed when the house shook.

"Mooooom!" she called, jumping up. The sky was

suddenly black. "Mooom! Daaadd!" Ro stumbled down the hallway. "Hello?" She ran as the tiles broke under her, the kitchen ceiling dropping to the ground.

"Where is she?" a bubbly voice called from the living room.

"I will never tell you!" her dad yelled. Was that smoke she was smelling?

"No!" The voice chimed again. "She has a destiny to fulfill."

Her mom was suddenly shielding her away.

"She will never be your scapegoat."

The yelling from the living room continued.

"Mom, what's going on?" They rushed through the splintering home.

"There's so much we haven't told you. So much we wanted to protect you from."

The house continued falling around them, covering everything in dust and soot.

"I'm sorry," her mom cried. "Sparrow, we love you so much."

"Mom, what's happening?" They were at the back door.

"Run, Sparrow! Run and never look back. Forget about us."

"Mom!"

Her mother flung the door open, pushing her daughter out of the crumbling entrance.

"Run Sparrow!" she yelled in desperation.

Bright colourful sparks flew, and dark figures in cloaks danced around the front of the home, hovering above the ground. Ro stumbled back, turning toward the edge of the false blackness, toward the daylight.

"Oh dear," the cheery voice from before chimed. "Are you lost, little birdy?"

Ro stumbled, turning away.

"AETERNUS SOMNUS!"

Everything went black.

"Sparrow, deep breaths." The withered old monarch hovered over her granddaughter.

"You're okay, you're safe."

She looked toward the older woman with wide eyes.

"The Nefarie"

"Yes, calm yourself first."

"No, they were there, they knew my dad. He had a screaming match with one of them. They destroyed our home; they hit me with a curse."

Elsina walked her out of the room. "Let's get some tea in you first. Something calming. Then we can talk about what you choose to do."

She looked at her grandmother questioningly.

"Stay here and you'll have lessons in sparring and magic to help against the Nefarie. It won't be easy, and many will hate you for what you are or might be." Elsina looked at her hard and stern. "You can return back to your world of course, but be warned, a war is coming. I fear even leaving won't protect you from it."

"I'm not running away. You have to promise me though, Elsina, to stop keeping me in the dark. I'm not a scared child. I'm a pissed daughter."

They walked further on, stepping into another elevator. "I want to learn how to control my magic. The Nefarie, they attacked us. Attacked me. Cursed my family. They're still after me."

"Yes, I can agree with you." Her grandmother nodded. "Perhaps we have kept you in the dark for too long. You're safe here though, they cannot hurt you. "

"I still need to be prepared."

"Wait." Her grandmother stared at her long and hard. "Sparrow, you must understand. The Nefarie are after you because you are a royal of mixed Elven and Fae blood. They have it in their head you have a power that can help them take over the mortal realm and return us to the old ways. Your parents, my son… they did not want this for you. Staying… taking this role… not going back to the human realm… it must be your choice. But I can offer you protection if you do choose to leave."

"Protection like they had…?"

Elsina looked down, ashamed. "I'm sorry about that… I can only offer you what power I have."

"What would the lessons be?"

"Understanding magical techniques, like most learn at the Halls of Ivy, but more specified to you."

"And fighting lessons?"

Elsina looked at her silently, evaluating as she held the doors open for her to leave the elevator. "Yes," she agreed, nodding solemnly. "If you decide to stay, then yes, you will have armoury lessons. Whatever you choose that you need. Along with diplomatic training."

They continued on, pausing before stepping into the warm dining area.

"Sparrow… I want you to think about this hard and long though."

"I AM."

Elsina nodded softly. "Still, you have until tomorrow to give me your answer. Either way, you'll tell me what you remember tonight. No one else. Now… let's present you for dinner."

They turned into an ostentatious room.

A large round table of soft stained wood, draped in a black silk cloth and covered with steaming food stood in the centre. Ace and Adyra stood, gesturing to a seat between them.

"I thought you might feel better in between your friends," Elsina said.

Ro hurried to join them. Sharing a smile, she started to draw out her seat, her brain bouncing with thoughts about how best to share what she'd learned with her friends.

"Ahem," a voice sang. "Is this her? Oh my goodness, it is!" A bouncing beauty glided in, dressed in green and purple hues.

Ace and Adyra stood then bowed once more.

"Oh up, up, come on, silly gooses," the woman gracefully chimed. "Are you her? Sparrow? Oh, of course you are!"

Elsina called from a few seats down. "Sparrow, let me introduce your Aunt Adelina. Princess in blood to Merwin and the court of Fae."

Adelina's lavender hair all but smothered her as she

pulled Ro in for a hug. "Move please." She slid Adyra down a seat. "I must sit by my long-lost niece!"

Ro sat next to her calmly, catching her aunt's golden eyes.

"Oh, I am so excited you are here. I can assist on your magic lessons and help with potions!"

"Adelina, Ro still hasn't decided her plan. Your aunt is the best of the best when it comes to potions," Elsina called out. "Now eat, the both of you. More catching up to do later, I'm sure"

"Oh, but you simply must stay. We can talk boys, or girls, and spells and clothes!" Adelina squealed, hugging Ro's arm tight as she rambled on and on down a twisting gleeful trail.

She no longer had Ro's attention though. Somewhere behind the grins and squeals of her aunt, a bubbling tinkling laugh sent shivers down her spine. Shivers that had nothing to do with the searing pain her wrist now experienced.

"Elsina," Ro called quietly, with a soft smile. All eyes turned to her calm demeanour.

"Yes, dear."

"You won't need to wait until tomorrow."

Adelina bounced cheerfully in her plush seat, and Ro turned toward her slinky grin. "I'll stay. Potions with Adelina sound splendid."

Through their cheers of merriment the earth did not shake, and the sky did not blacken. Yet Ro knew that sitting next to her aunt did stir one thing: her rage.

ACKNOWLEDGEMENTS

My people (you know who you are) - Your belief in me is either bizarrely hopeful or semi delulu—either way, I'm grateful. I owe you all a massive coffee.

Momosa - The Lorelai to my Rory. For being my very first editor in life and the one who taught me that a good story always pairs well with a killer soundtrack. Your support of all my creative endeavours made the world a less scary place when I chose to share them.

Nana and Papa - Because of your creative spirits, short stories told around a campfire, and made-up lyrics on the strings of a guitar, I am the storyteller I am today. Your lessons and love live on through all of us, and this book is, in part, because of you both.

To my love - You helped me give Sparrow the wings to fly. Thank you for listening to my continuous rewrites and endless ideas, for the many hours of excitement and support, and for pushing me to finish just one more chapter when I edged towards procrastinating this tale away. Here's to all the adventures we've shared and those yet to come, and of course a hormaly dream or two; I love you!

Sparrow will be back...

ABOUT THE AUTHOR

April Sunshine is a fantasy bookworm originally from Florida, who loves art, history, and studying creating writing. A globetrotter with a passion for adventure, she can either be found travelling with her nose in a novel or listening to the rain with a hot coffee in hand while writing a book of her own.

www.ingramcontent.com/pod-product-compliance
Lightning Source LLC
Chambersburg PA
CBHW061123310726
48974CB00002B/660

9 781990 336850